"Lacey, have you done this before?"

Ethan asked as understanding dawned on his face. He rolled off her, and sat up on the edge of the bed. Then he turned and gently did up the buttons on her blouse.

She blushed red-hot. "I'm thirty years old," she said. "I want you," she whispered fiercely.

"Not like this," he said gruffly. "You don't even know me."

Didn't know him? How could he think that? How could she not know him when she had seen him tame a horse with his touch, and gentle her charges with his voice? How could she not know him when she had ridden through the snow with him, and felt the warmth of his hands? When she had stood in a bathroom still steamy from his shower? How could she have watched the steely gray of his eyes soften with tenderness and not know him?

She knew him. And she wanted to know all of him.

Dear Reader,

Compelling, emotionally charged stories featuring honorable heroes, strong heroines and the deeply rooted conflicts they must overcome to arrive at a happily-ever-after are what make a Silhouette Romance novel come alive. Look no further than this month's offerings for stories to sweep you away....

In *Johnny's Pregnant Bride,* the engaging continuation of Carolyn Zane's THE BRUBAKER BRIDES, an about-to-be-married cattle rancher honorably claims another woman— and another man's baby—as his own. This month's VIRGIN BRIDES title by Martha Shields shows that when *The Princess and the Cowboy* agree to a marriage of convenience, neither suspects the other's real identity...or how difficult *not* falling in love will be! In *Truly, Madly, Deeply,* Elizabeth August delivers a powerful transformation tale, in which a vulnerable woman finds her inner strength and outward beauty through the love of a tough-yet-tender single dad and his passel of kids.

And Then He Kissed Me by Teresa Southwick shows the romantic aftermath of a surprising kiss between best friends who'd been determined to stay that way. A runaway bride at a crossroads finds that *Weddings Do Come True* when the right man comes along in this uplifting novel by Cara Colter. And rounding out the month is Karen Rose Smith with a charming story whose title says it all: *Wishes, Waltzes and a Storybook Wedding.*

Enjoy this month's titles—and keep coming back to Romance, a series guaranteed to touch *every* woman's heart.

Mary-Theresa Hussey

Mary-Theresa Hussey
Senior Editor

Please address questions and book requests to:
Silhouette Reader Service
U.S.: 3010 Walden Ave., P.O. Box 1325, Buffalo, NY 14269
Canadian: P.O. Box 609, Fort Erie, Ont. L2A 5X3

WEDDINGS DO COME TRUE

Cara Colter

Silhouette

R O M A N C E™

Published by Silhouette Books

America's Publisher of Contemporary Romance

To my dear friend,
Marilyn Breckenridge

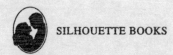 SILHOUETTE BOOKS

ISBN 0-373-19406-4

WEDDINGS DO COME TRUE

Copyright © 1999 by Cara Colter

Visit us at www.romance.net

Printed in U.S.A.

Books by Cara Colter

Silhouette Romance

Dare To Dream #491
Baby in Blue #1161
Husband in Red #1243
The Cowboy, the Baby and the Bride-to-Be #1319
Truly Daddy #1363
A Bride Worth Waiting For #1388
Weddings Do Come True #1406

CARA COLTER

shares ten acres in the wild Kootenay region of British Columbia with the man of her dreams, three children, two horses, a cat with no tail and a golden retriever who answers best to "bad dog." She loves reading, writing and the woods in winter (no bears). She says life's delights include an automatic garage door opener and the skylight over the bed that allows her to see the stars at night.

She also says, "I have not lived a neat and tidy life, and used to envy those who did. Now I see my struggles as having given me a deep appreciation of life, and of love, that I hope I succeed in passing on through the stories that I tell."

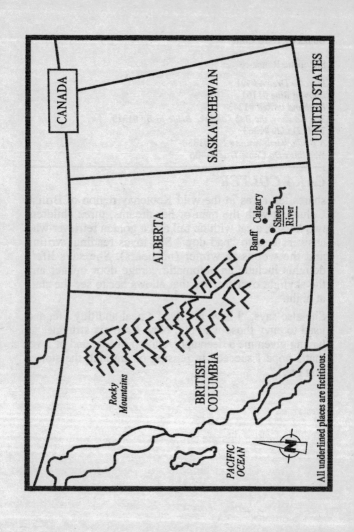

All underlined places are fictitious.

Chapter One

Ethan Black gazed out the window above the kitchen sink. He was buried up to his elbows in suds. The last light was fading from the sky; leafless trees and snow-capped evergreens were stark black silhouettes against the sunset's final streaks of orange and pink. A cow lowed, the sound deep and melodious.

Slivers of light still illuminated the tops of the rolling hills that stretched to the far horizon. He could no longer see the lonely ribbon of road that wound from miles away, down over Sheep Creek Ridge, through the shadowed valley and up here to his home on Black's Bluff, but at night like this, he could see headlights coming from four miles off.

But there were no pinpoints of light heralding the arrival of the cavalry.

He frowned. His aging hired hand, Gumpy, should have been back from Calgary by now. With the reinforcements.

Reinforcement. Mrs. Betty-Anne Bishop.

Tearing his hopeful gaze from the place the headlights would first appear crowning the crest of the ridge, he looked down at the contents of the sink with disgust. He was doing dishes. Lots and lots of dishes. Once upon a time, doing dishes had meant turning on the hot water tap and giving a single plate a quick swish through it. Two plates, if Gumpy joined him.

Once upon a time. Only two weeks ago. How could two weeks seem so long?

Peals of shrill laughter erupted from down the hall, and he closed his eyes. That was how.

He leaned back from the sink, trying not to drip too many suds, and peered down the darkened hallway. A light was on in his bedroom at the end of the passageway.

The two children were jumping up and down on his bed, squealing with hyenalike glee.

They were twins, and though not identical, the resemblance between them was strong and striking. Both had short dark hair, though not nearly as dark as his and not as heavy. Doreen's eyes were blue; Danny's were the Black eyes, gray as slate. Both of them had cheekbones that only hinted at their grandmother's—his mother's—Sarcee Indian blood. Tsuu-T'ina, Gumpy's voice corrected him inside his head. Gumpy would be disgusted to know Ethan was relieved his niece and nephew would not be taunted through their school years as he had been. Called half-breed and worse. Driven, later on, to prove himself. To prove that he was just as good as anybody else. No, better. Stronger. Tougher. Wilder. More fearless.

He watched the children for a moment longer, thinking either of them was going to bounce one of their stocky little bodies right off the bed. He should tell them to settle down.

On the other hand, they weren't fighting.

He turned back to the chore at hand. The morning and lunch dishes finally done, he shook his hands over the sink. Reminding himself the end was in sight, he went and cleared the supper dishes off the table.

"I hate this, Unca," his five-year-old niece, Doreen, had told him a half hour ago.

"Eat it anyway."

Her huge cornflower-blue eyes had filled with silent tears. They had the oddest way of filling, from the bottom, like a clear glass fish bowl filling up. Or maybe everybody's eyes filled up that way before they bawled and he'd just never had a chance to see it up close before.

Thank God.

Needless to say, she had not eaten one bite of the prime T-bone on the plate. Or the baked potato, which admittedly had not been cooked all the way through. She had nibbled a single leaf of lettuce, which, from the level of energy she was now demonstrating on his bed, had sufficiently nourished her.

He dropped the dishes in the sink. He had to bend in an awkward way, right from the small of his back, to get at the dishes, and he was starting to ache from it. Of course, his aching back might also have a little something to do with a long-ago bull named Desire. His aches and scars—and there were many of them considering he had barely broken thirty—were mostly named after bulls he'd met over a seven-year stint as a pro-rodeo cowboy.

Not one moment of which had been as frightening as the moment Doreen and her twin brother, Danny, had stepped into the airport waiting area, holding hands, their names pinned to their coats, their eyes huge and frightened.

He heard a thud as one of them tumbled off the bed.

He waited for the howl and felt his muscles actually un-bunching when it didn't come. A moment later the springs were again squeakily protesting each jump.

They weren't frightened anymore. Maybe they never had been. Maybe that had just been his own fear reflected in their eyes. Imagine a man who had spent most of his youth and much of his adult life on top of two thousand pounds of writhing, raging bull getting an attack of nerves when confronted with two small scraps of humanity who couldn't weigh more than eighty pounds combined. It was humiliating.

His sister, Nancy, and her husband, Andrew, were medical missionaries in a country called Rotanbonga. He still couldn't pronounce it correctly. The twins had been born there, and he'd been quite satisfied to monitor their progress from a distance. His chief duty as uncle had been to remember to get their Christmas parcel in the mail by the end of September. Every year he sent a teddy bear and a doll, thanking God for the Sears catalogue, so that he didn't have to shop for these highly embarrassing items in person.

But a few weeks ago he'd gotten an extremely panicky call from his usually unflappable sister. The connection was terrible, but he understood her to say that an epidemic, the name of which he could not pronounce, was sweeping the towns of their adopted homeland. It wasn't safe for the kids to stay, but Nancy and Andrew felt they couldn't possibly leave when so many lives now relied on their medical expertise.

What was an uncle supposed to say in those circum-stances? I've got a ranch to run?

Of course, at the time when he'd said yes, he'd had no idea two five-year-olds were going to keep him from run-ning his ranch. Keep him so busy and exhausted, he fell into bed at night feeling as if he'd wrestled, branded and inoculated several thousand head of cattle singlehandedly.

"Come on, Gumpy," he implored the dark road.

He hoped the old truck hadn't given out somewhere along the way. Gumpy always kept a roll of electrical tape and spare parts on hand and could bring about major miracles on that old heap of junk, but still, it wouldn't make a good first impression on Mrs. Bishop.

She might not be happy standing in the dark on the side of the road in the biting November cold watching Gumpy cheerfully gluing his pride and joy back together.

And he wanted nothing more than for Mrs. Bishop to be happy.

Mrs. Betty-Anne Bishop was his neighbor's cousin. Her name had come to him after he'd put out some panicky feelers to friends and neighbors.

That was three days after the twins had arrived. The laundry seemed to be multiplying on its own on the laundry room floor, the cattle needed to be dewormed, and Danny and Doreen had not yet revealed to him if they understood English.

He'd interviewed Mrs. Bishop by telephone. She was fifty-seven and had raised four children of her own.

None of whom were in jail.

Which was good enough for him.

It hadn't fazed him that she lived in Ottawa, fifteen hundred miles away, either. He'd paid the short-notice, no-discount airfare to Calgary without blinking.

"It's mine!" Doreen screamed.

"Isn't!" Danny yelled back.

Ethan sighed and closed his eyes.

Now they were fighting. In some ways he'd liked it better before they decided to let him know they spoke English.

He leaned back from the sink again and looked down the hall to his bedroom. They were still smack-dab in the middle of his bed, engaged in a furious tug-of-war over his cowboy hat. Didn't they know a man's hat was sacred?

"Hey!" he hollered.

Doreen started, and dropped her hold on the hat. She fell on her plump bottom and looked accusingly down the hall at him. Even from here he could see her large blue eyes filling up with tears.

Wringing out the dishcloth with a little more vigor than was absolutely necessary, he said a word that would have given his sister a heart attack, and headed down the hall.

A few minutes later, Doreen tucked under one arm and Danny under the other, Ethan settled on the couch. They snuggled into him, and the opening credits of Toy Story came on.

"How many times have we watched this, Unca?" Doreen asked him happily.

"Twenty-seven," he informed her grimly.

She sighed blissfully. Danny sang the opening song robustly. Ethan felt his eyelids growing heavier and heavier.

It seemed like only minutes later he jerked awake. But the TV was now playing plain blue, and Danny and Doreen were fast asleep, their heads on his chest, Danny snoring softly and Doreen drooling a little pool of saliva all over the front of his shirt.

If it hadn't been for the drool, he might have thought he was dreaming.

Because there was an angel in the room with them.

She was absolutely beautiful. Her hair was thick and long, as golden as liquid honey, half piled on top of her head, and half falling around her face and shoulders. She

had beautiful dark brown eyes, high cheekbones, a
shapely nose, a mouth from which the lipstick had long
ago worn off, but that still looked luscious.

Lipstick? Since when did angels wear lipstick?

He blinked, and gave his head a shake.

Since when did angels wear little pink silk suits, the
color of cotton candy? The skirt showed Ethan enough
long, shapely leg to make his mouth go dry.

"Honey, we're home," Gumpy said with a familiar
cackle.

Ethan snapped his gaze to him. Gumpy, his wispy
white hair framing his wrinkled copper-colored face,
looked inordinately pleased with himself.

Ethan lifted the children's heads off his chest and
slipped out from under them. Stepping over the coffee
table, he ignored Gumpy, and stared down at the beautiful
intruder.

"Who the hell are you?" he asked, his voice rougher
than it needed to be in defense against those legs.

Lacey McCade stared up at the cowboy with awe. He
was at least three inches taller than her own five feet nine
inches. There was pure power in the strong lines of his
face, in the high cut of his cheekbones, in the faint cleft
of his chin, the straight line of his nose. His hair was
thick and black as night and cut very short. His lips were
full and faintly parted, and his eyelashes were long and
sooty. His skin glowed with faint copper tones, and she
knew he must be at least partly Native American.

His build was lean and hard. He had his shirtsleeves
rolled up, and she could see the sinewy muscle of his
lower arms, the strength in his large wrists. He flexed a
hand impatiently, and her eyes were drawn momentarily
to a thick scar that snaked around the base of his thumb.

He was wearing a denim shirt, and his shoulders and chest were broad beneath it.

Two ax handles wide, Lacey remembered her secretary saying once, giggling at a carpenter's shoulders, as they passed a construction site on their way to an office luncheon.

Lacey remembered thinking at the time, Who in Los Angeles would know the first thing about ax handles? But she was a long way from Los Angeles now, and looking at those enormously broad shoulders, it fit.

His legs were very long, encased in old denim that looked as soft as felt, and clung to the large muscles of his thighs.

His eyes were astonishing, even in anger. They were gray and clear as cold mountain water. Not that anybody in Los Angeles would know anything about that, either.

"Hi," she said nervously.

"Who the hell are you?" he repeated.

He had every right to be angry. Lacey shot a look at her rescuer, Gumpy. Or was she rescuing *him?* It had all seemed so simple at the airport.

She had just gotten off the phone to Keith who had not taken the news she was canceling the wedding very well. In fact, he had said he would get on the next flight and they would "talk."

She hadn't been in the mood for talking, and had decided to hide out in a hotel room. But after thirty-two phone calls, it was apparent to her that every hotel room in the whole city of Calgary was being used for an international convention of plumbers. Who would have known plumbers had conventions?

And then this wonderful old man had been standing in front of her, in faded jeans and a denim jacket. He was Native American, his skin warm and wrinkled copper, his eyes black as coal, his hair long and free and wispy as white smoke.

She had liked his eyes, because despite the nervous twisting of his hat in his hands, his eyes had been utterly calm, peaceful. In his eyes had been a deep knowing.

About everything. The secrets of life and the universe. *Her* secrets.

"Are you the nanny?" he'd asked shyly, revealing a gap where his two front teeth should have been.

She'd contemplated that for a moment. What she was, was a lawyer, one who had never had an impulsive moment before today. Today when, instead of driving to her law firm's office in downtown Los Angeles after a particularly brutal session with a difficult client, she had taken the off-ramp to the airport, surveyed the flights out and chosen Calgary.

For no reason at all, really.

Unless you counted the fact that once, as a little girl, she had wanted very badly to go there for their world-famous rodeo, the Calgary Stampede.

And then some complete stranger with lovable eyes had asked her if she was a nanny, and some deep warmth had spread within her. Of course, she would have said no if he hadn't spoken again.

"If you're not the nanny, I guess I'm in a heap of trouble," the old man had said sadly.

But his eyes had said no such thing. They twinkled at her as if they were about to share a wonderful joke. They invited her to say yes to the adventure. He *knew* she was not a nanny.

It felt as though Lacey was in a "heap of trouble" herself. Still, her utterly responsible voice ordered her indignantly not to do anything crazy. Anything else crazy. She shushed it.

The truth was she wanted, for once in her very ordinary life, to be crazy. She wanted to be impetuous and spontaneous. She wanted life to at least have the possibility of something wonderful and unpredictable happening.

And after she'd had that, her small taste of life on the wild side, a breath or two of pure freedom, she would probably be perfectly content to go home and marry Keith. Perfectly.

"I am a nanny," she told her unlikely angel, holding out her hand to him.

He took it, and any doubt she had was gone instantly. His grip was strong and warm and reassuring. "I lost the paper with your name on it, miss."

She hesitated, knowing when she said her name he was going to realize his error. And the adventure would be over just like that. She'd get on the next plane and go home.

She had been aware of holding her breath as she said, "Lacey. My name's Lacey McCade."

But his smile had nearly swallowed his face. "Nelson," he'd told her, "Nelson Go-Up-the-Mountain." When she told him she had never heard such a beautiful name, he had ducked his head with endearing shyness. "Shucks, just call me Gumpy."

Lacey had never heard anyone say "Shucks" before. She wanted to ask him all about the children, but remembered she was likely supposed to know.

"Your luggage?" he'd asked her.

"Lost." She felt guilty lying to him, but really that one word could mean just about anything. And it suddenly occurred to her that the turnoff to the airport earlier had been very much about things lost. Some part of herself was lost.

"We'll find it," he'd said reassuringly.

And looking at him, she'd believed it. And knew he was not talking about luggage any more than she was.

Now, facing the man in front of her, her choice seemed silly rather than adventurous.

Even sleeping, with those two adorable children nestled trustingly into him, there had been nothing vulnerable about this man. He had looked rugged and 100 percent pure male.

"Mind your manners, Ethan," Gumpy told him mildly, which earned the older man a look that might have sent a lesser man scuttling for cover. "This is our new nanny."

"The hell she is."

Certainly she was glancing around for a place to hide.

But with one more dismissive look to her, Ethan turned to Gumpy. "What have you gone and done?"

"Just what you told me," Gumpy said, "gone to the airport and picked up the nanny."

"Fifty-seven. I told you Betty-Anne was fifty-seven years old. Nobody fifty-seven looks like this. This girl isn't a day over—" cool gray eyes scanned her "—twenty-five."

"Woman," she corrected him. "Thirty."

He glared at her briefly, then shifted his attention away from her again.

"Gumpy, start talking." The cowboy's voice was low and lethal. Just like the rest of him, there was barely leashed power in that voice. "Where's Mrs. Bishop?"

Behind him the children stirred on the couch. She watched them, in their sleep, reach out for and find each other. She felt a stab of tenderness for them.

"This is the only nanny I could find at the airport," Gumpy said, not intimidated. "And believe you me, I looked."

"Anybody looking at her can see she's not a nanny. We need somebody who can cook and clean and look after kids, Gumpy, not an expert in shades of fingernail polish."

She looked at the fingernails in question, rather than meet the steady, stripping look in his eyes when he glanced back her way. Her nails were quite long, the very same shade as her suit, a fact she had taken some pleasure in this morning.

When she had been a completely different person.

"Doreen and Danny will like her," Gumpy said.

"I hope you're not suggesting she stay."

She looked up from her fingernails to see Gumpy nod, once, with grave dignity.

The cool, angry note in Ethan's voice as he bit out a single word woke the children. They struggled to sit up, rubbing their eyes, taking her in with only mild curiosity. Then they slipped off the couch and disappeared down the hall.

"Don't touch my hat," Ethan called over his shoulder, though he did not turn around.

The children giggled and broke into a run that did not bode well for his hat, though at the moment she could not imagine anyone who valued their lives defying him.

But Gumpy did defy him. "I think she should stay."

"You crazy old coot! She is not staying. You are putting her back in that truck and taking her back wherever you found her."

"So," Gumpy said softly, "now I'm a crazy old coot. But when you want something, it's Grandfather."

"You're his grandfather?" Lacey asked Gumpy with surprise.

"No!" Ethan snapped.

"For the People, Grandfather is a term that denotes

respect," Gumpy said softly, his dark eyes locked on the gray ones of the younger man.

To her immense surprise, Ethan looked down first. A small muscle jerked angrily in his jaw. But when he looked up again at Gumpy, the flash of fury was gone from his eyes, though they were as cool and as unnervingly steady as ever.

"She can't stay," he said quietly.

"He's right," Lacey said, moving to Gumpy and putting her hand on his sleeve. "Of course I can't stay. I've made a dreadful mistake. I'll go. Really."

Gumpy studied her face, saw the resolve in it and sighed.

The little girl danced into the room. "Gumpy, I flushed your keys down the toilet."

Ethan said that word again, so that Lacey just barely heard it. Not a very nice word at all.

"Don't you just love flush toilets?" the little girl asked, looking right up at her.

She had the most beautiful blue eyes, Lacey thought, and exquisite bone structure, very like her uncle's. Short dark hair scattered around a cherubic face. Out of the corner of her eye, Lacey saw Gumpy struggling to suppress his laughter. His thin shoulders were shaking.

"I do," Lacey said, though she had to admit she had never given the topic a single thought in her entire life. "I like flush toilets very much."

The other little imp materialized, and looked up at her with eyes amazingly like his uncle's. "I'm Danny."

"Hi," Lacey said.

"And I'm Doreen," the other one said.

Ethan was not being sidetracked by introductions. "You can take my truck," he said grimly to Gumpy.

"You'll be back in plenty of time for us to use it to feed cattle."

Lacey looked at Gumpy with concern. Surely he would not be expected to drive back and forth all night and then feed cattle in the morning?

"Never mind," Ethan said, evidently reaching the same conclusion. For a moment in his eyes a barrier came down, and she could see his affectionate concern for the old man outweigh his substantial irritation. "I'll take her."

He strode out of the room, and it was as if something went with him. Energy. Light. Lacey realized his physical nearness had made her edgy, aware of something beating, pulsing, deep within her.

Danny and Doreen raced around the room and then disappeared down the hallway.

Lacey studied the living room. It was only slightly homier than the kitchen she had come through earlier. The couch looked worn but comfortable. A bright scatter rug was underneath it, no doubt to keep feet warm on icy winter nights. The coffee table, a beautiful old scarred wooden trunk, held a cup of coffee, half-full, and a well-thumbed book that looked like a medical manual on cattle. There were no pictures on the walls.

Keith, she knew, would hate this room. His taste ran to authentic Persian rugs and antique oriental vases. But she found herself drawn to it, to the lack of clutter, to the simplicity.

She glanced, covertly, at the four movies lined up under the television, wondering what they would tell her of the man who lived here. *Toy Story, Teenage Mutant Ninja Turtles, Dances with Wolves* and *Chris Irwin, Horse Whispering Demystified.* Gumpy shuffled over and sat on the couch, looking peaceful and unperturbed, but she felt driven to apologize anyway.

"I'm sorry, Gumpy," she said softly, "I never should have let it go this far."

He just smiled, that wise and knowing smile she had come to like very much.

They heard a drawer slam in the kitchen.

"Where the hell are my keys?"

From a different part of the house, Lacey heard breathless giggles.

Ethan must have heard them, too. Because the silence was suddenly very silent. She could hear the fridge motor.

"Doreen?" he called. "Danny?"

Silence.

"Where are my keys?"

Hushed giggles.

Lacey turned to Gumpy and widened her eyes. She mouthed, "The toilet?"

He nodded and she waited for an explosion, but none came.

Ethan came back into the living room. He sank down on the couch and closed his eyes for a long moment. He looked tired and discouraged, much, she thought, how she must have looked when Gumpy found her at the airport.

"You probably can't even cook," he muttered in her direction.

"You haven't eaten until you've had my vegetarian chili," she told him proudly.

"Vegetarian?" he said with flat dislike.

Even loyal Gumpy was looking at her with distress. "Vegetarian?"

They heard a toilet flush and then flush again, followed by childish laughter.

"My life," Ethan said, slowly and deliberately, "could not possibly get any worse than it is at this moment."

She felt it was wise to say nothing. Apparently so did Gumpy.

"Miss?" Ethan said, opening one gray eye and looking at her.

"Ms.," she corrected him.

His sigh of long suffering said his life had just gotten worse. "You're on a cattle ranch," he told her, reclosing his eyes. "As in beef. We promote the edibility of red meat."

"Oh."

The phone rang, and for a long time it seemed as if both men planned to ignore it.

"You know who that is, don't you?" Ethan asked Gumpy.

"Not a clue."

"It's a hopping-mad fifty-seven-year-old woman who has successfully raised four children on a diet of meat and potatoes." Except for the hopping-mad part, he sounded distinctly wistful.

He unfolded himself from the couch and went and got the phone.

Chapter Two

The phone was wall mounted in the hallway. Ethan picked it up and looked back at the pink suit settling herself on his sofa. She crossed one long, slender leg over the other one. That suit really said it all.

This was no nanny.

This was trouble. Capital-*T* trouble.

He deliberately turned his back on her, but was annoyed that the picture of her did not leave his mind. He tried to concentrate on what Derrick Bishop was telling him.

His mother, Mrs. Bishop, was in the hospital in Ottawa. Something about a bad spill on some ice on the sidewalk outside the airport that had left her with a broken hip.

Knowing he was being a selfish SOB, all Ethan could think was that the cavalry was not coming after all.

Unless you counted *her*. He hung up the phone and turned back, using the darkness of the hall to study her.

The cavalry she was not.

Cavalries did not come in that particular shade of pink.

Her skin was faintly golden, and the suit was lightweight. He figured she did not come from a Northern climate. The suit really was an engineering marvel. It looked businesslike, but it also clung and hinted.

Ethan Black had pictured Betty-Anne Bishop to be the approximate size and shape of a refrigerator. Nothing had prepared him for *this*.

He deeply resented the flash of heat he felt deep in his belly when his lovely intruder flung a heavy tress of wayward hair over a softly rounded shoulder, even though it confirmed the absolute wisdom of getting rid of her. Fast.

The truth was he'd had lots of experience with beautiful women. Win a few buckles, ride a few bulls, and you were suddenly irresistible. Barbie doll beauty hadn't impressed him all those years ago, and it didn't impress him now, or at least not the part of him he listened to.

Now, brains, he thought, that impressed him in a woman.

And he could tell this girl—make that Ms. Woman— was short in the smarts department. Who else would get in a truck with a toothless old man they knew nothing about?

He hoped to God she wasn't a hooker.

He considered that, watching her with narrowed eyes. The suit was very expensive looking and very proper. If it weren't for the color—and for the fact he knew she'd taken a ride with a stranger to an unknown destination— he might think high-powered executive type. She smiled at something Gumpy said. The smile was warm and open.

But that didn't alter the fact she was an impostor. She had lied to Gumpy.

Expensively dressed. Beautiful. Desperate. A woman in trouble.

He did not need any more troubles. Not of his own or

anybody else's, either. Double trouble had arrived here
two weeks ago, and Danny and Doreen were his absolute
limit. She had to go. He was still the boss around here,
not Gumpy.

Of course, there was the little matter of the keys. If he
took the toilet apart tonight, a prospect that blackened his
already-black mood, Gumpy could take her back to Calgary first thing in the morning. He could feed the cattle
on his own. He cursed the early skiff of snow that added
four hours of feeding cattle to his daily workload. Six, if
Gumpy weren't here.

What was he going to do with the kids? The thought
of taking them with him to feed the cattle was enough to
raise the hair on the back of his neck. He thought of
sending them with Gumpy, but there wouldn't be enough
seat belts in Gumpy's truck, not that Gumpy would go
for it if there were. Pulling rank only went so far with
his old hand. Of course, Gumpy was more than a hand,
and he knew it.

More even than a friend. A link to ways long forgotten.

He went back into the living room. Danny and Doreen
streaked by, his hat down around Doreen's chin, Danny
riding hard on a broomstick.

"What's your name?" Ethan asked the woman.

He knew before she answered, he was going to hate
her name. He knew she would have a name like Tiffany,
or Jade, or Charity.

"Lacey," she said evenly, "Lacey McCade."

Bingo. Not a sensible name like Mary or Betty.

"Mrs. Bishop broke her hip," he said to Gumpy.
"She's not coming."

Gumpy beamed as if he'd just won the lottery. The
kids screeched through, squeezing between the coffee table and the couch.

But she reached out an arm and stopped Doreen and then caught up Danny. "You can help me bake cookies tomorrow if you go quietly and put on your pajamas."

Tomorrow?

"What kind?" Danny demanded.

"What kind do you like?"

Ethan glared at her. *Tomorrow?*

"Chocolate chip," they said together.

"We don't have chocolate chips," he said. Not that she was going to be here long enough to bake cookies.

"I can do it before I go," she told him levelly, as if she could read his mind. "It only takes half an hour or so." And then as if that settled it, she smiled at the kids, a smile so radiant it almost melted the caution he felt. Almost. "Do you like oatmeal cookies?" she asked them.

They hooted their approval, just as if they fully intended to earn their cookies by quietly going and putting on their pajamas.

"Oatmeal?" she asked him.

He nodded curtly, folded his arms over his chest, tried to suppress his surprise—and annoyance—when Doreen and Danny regarded her solemnly for a moment, and then marched off silently to put on their PJ's.

Gumpy looked smug.

"She's not staying," Ethan bit out.

"Well, she's gotta stay tonight. Unless you got a spare set of keys made after we ran those ones through the baler."

He hadn't, and Gumpy knew it.

"I'm taking the toilet apart right now. The keys are probably caught in the trap."

"Well, I ain't waiting up for you to do it."

Ethan saw he was being unreasonable. He'd already decided they would have to take her back tomorrow. It would be too late to do it after he'd rescued the keys. And he still had to get those kids to bed.

But the kids marched out in their pajamas, asked a couple of anxious questions about cookie baking and then asked her if she'd tuck them in.

Not him, the one who'd cooked for them and watched *Toy Story* with them twenty-seven times and washed their mountain of dishes, and let them play with his damned hat.

Nope. Her. The impostor.

"Well, now she's gotta stay and make cookies," Gumpy pronounced with satisfaction when she'd left the room, one hand firmly in the grasp of each child. "Promises are important."

Actually, though he wouldn't admit it out loud, that would work out fine. He could get up early with Gumpy and feed the cattle, she could watch the kids and make cookies and then leave right after lunch. Not perfect, but workable.

Whatever had driven her here, he was pretty sure she was not the type who would be rummaging through the house looking for stuff to steal.

Not that he had anything worth taking. Unless you counted Chris Irwin's video. The VCR was Gumpy's.

"Been a long time since I had cookies that didn't come out of a bag," Gumpy said, getting up and stretching. "I'm goin'. Do you think she'll cook us breakfast? I'm fair tired of instant porridge."

Ethan was tired of instant porridge, too, especially the way Gumpy made it, with hot water straight out of the tap. But if he complained, he'd end up with breakfast duty. So he just said, "Get real. Does she look like the type who cooks breakfast?"

"She does to me," Gumpy said stubbornly, and moved by him. "She's going to make cookies, ain't she?"

Ethan followed him and watched as the older man went down the stairs to the landing and bent over his boots, continuing to mutter the whole time.

"I bet the cookies won't be any good, anyway," Ethan said.

Gumpy mumbled something.

"I didn't catch that," he finally said, knowing he was taking the bait.

Gumpy straightened. "I think we should make a bet. If she cooks breakfast, she stays."

"Gumpy, I don't even know where you found her."

"At the airport, just like you said."

"We don't know anything about her."

"Just look in her eyes."

"She lied to you. She's no nanny."

"Neither are you. I don't hold it against you."

"But I never said I was," he said with elaborate patience.

"I bet she can do the job."

"And I bet I'm going to be asked to be the guest conductor for the Calgary Philharmonic."

"She's supposed to be here." He opened the door and cold air blasted in.

Gumpy considered himself to be something of a mystic. He was right about things often enough that Ethan had stopped laughing. He eyed the old man warily.

"If she cooks breakfast tomorrow, you should ask her to stay," Gumpy said stubbornly.

"Only if it's good," Ethan said dryly. Not much danger on either count, but Gumpy looked pleased, like a fisherman who had a strong nibble. "Maybe you should stay in the house tonight."

Gumpy shook his head obstinately and went out.

Ethan turned back into the house, which was unbelievably silent. If he strained, he could just hear the soft murmur of her voice. He turned on the radio to drown it out. Fighting weariness, he turned off the water main and began to scoop the water out of the toilet.

"The kids are asleep. I'm going to go to bed."

By now he had out a wrench and was unbolting the bowl from the floor. He looked out at her from where he was twisted beneath the tank. She was standing in the door watching him as though he was performing heart surgery. "Yeah. Sure. First door on the right."

"I figured it out. The lace doily on the dresser was a dead giveaway."

He glanced at her sharply. Was she smarter than she looked? He'd put that little scrap of lace out to make it look welcoming for Mrs. Bishop. It was the only doodad in his house.

"Sleep in tomorrow," he suggested. After all, he had a bet to win. Not that he had much in the way of breakfast makings around, anyway. He hadn't really had time to properly stock groceries. He had eggs, cereal and instant porridge. Good luck turning that into anything special.

Gumpy wouldn't consider boiling the water for the instant porridge cooking, would he? Contemplating that, he went back to work.

An hour later, the keys rescued and the toilet bowl reanchored to the floor, he showered, checked on his niece and nephew and walked by Lacey McCade's firmly shut door.

It occurred to him she hadn't had a single piece of luggage with her.

Which made him wonder again where she had come

from and why. It also made him wonder what she was sleeping in.

Lacey lay awake in the inky darkness. The bed was narrow and lumpy. She wondered what he was sleeping in. Boxers?

She could feel herself coloring to the roots of her hair. Which was a mess.

She was in a strange man's house, under false pretenses, thinking decadent thoughts. What had happened to her? She was not the same woman who had gotten up this morning, calmly eaten her toast and jam, and headed for work.

Just this morning she had been the fast-rising woman lawyer, preparing for the wedding of the century, and the life of acquiring the stuff—the beach house, the car.

The kids, she realized, had never come up.

A foolish thing not to have discussed with the man you were going to marry—presumably the catch of the season.

Lacey replayed the conversation she'd had with Keith, from the airport at Calgary, rather than think any more thoughts about the cowboy in his boxer shorts. Or lack thereof.

"Keith," she had said, watching a 747 lumber along the runway, looking as if it would never have the power to take off, "Cancel the wedding."

At the precise moment she had said those words, the plane was suddenly in the air, its huge body soaring upward at an impossibly steep angle.

She surprised herself. Her voice sounded firm and sure and uncompromising.

Silence. Then, "Lacey?"

"Cancel the wedding," she repeated, more strongly than before.

She pictured him behind his desk, his tie undone, his blond head bowed over some paperwork, though she thought she probably had his undivided attention now.

"I can't cancel the wedding," he sputtered. "It's three weeks away. It's going to be *the* wedding." Long fingers would be scraping back his hair, his handsome features would be marred by a frown, the wrinkles deep in his forehead.

Lacey turned from the bank of windows. The plane was now a speck in the distance. She took a deep breath. On the other side of the pay phone she was using stood a beautiful statue, cast in bronze, protected by a glass case. It was of a cowboy standing quietly beside a horse that dipped its head to water. Something about it had made her ache with an emotion she did not understand.

But that had something to do with the word *the*. Why did it have to be *the* wedding?

She would have settled for a wedding. For ordinary things.

She snorted at herself. Since when?

Since precisely three hours ago, when the off-ramp to the airport had beckoned to her so bewitchingly she could not say no.

"Where are you?" Keith demanded.

"I don't think that's important."

"Area code 403," he read off his call display.

Her eyes rested on the bronze again. When she was a child, she had begged her father to consider the Stampede as a vacation possibility. There had never been money for exotic holidays, though. Not that her father would have considered a rodeo exotic.

Lacey wondered about taking it in while she was here.

Then some long-forgotten part of her recalled the Stampede was in the summer. July? And summer was long past here.

Listening, she could hear Keith on the other end of the line, thumbing through papers. The telephone book, she guessed bleakly.

"Canada," he crowed. "Alberta. Lacey, what are you doing in Alberta?"

"I don't know," she'd answered truthfully.

And she didn't. She only knew that when she had seen the airport sign, she had been compelled to obey something within her that told her to go. To go now. Before it was too late.

For what, she was not sure.

Keith was handsome, gloriously so. And wildly successful in his own right, quite separate from the old family wealth he came from. "A young man going to the very top," her father had pronounced with grave approval after meeting him for the first time.

And, of course, Lacey had her own career, and though it was not quite as illustrious as Keith's, between the two of them they were well on their way.

Again, her eyes had been drawn to the bronze cowboy. So still.

Of course he was still, she chided herself with annoyance. He was bronze.

"Lacey, what's the matter?"

Keith was trying so hard for a tender note, but she could picture him glancing at his watch. And she could certainly hear the edge of impatience in his voice. The wedding was about to go up in smoke because of a whim. *Her* whim. Keith did not like whims.

He liked things organized. Predictable. Perfect.

"I can't go through with it," she whispered. "I can't."

"There's no such word as *can't*." This was an expression Keith had picked up at one of the motivational seminars the company had sponsored.

"I'm having some doubts." The details on the bronze made it very lifelike. The bronze cowboy had his back to her, and when she was done on the phone she would go look at the front of him. Still, even from the back, how he was standing said so much. Weariness in the slope of his shoulders but pride, too.

"What kind of doubts? Why now? The time for doubts was six months ago. A year."

She knew she had failed to have her doubts on schedule. Before the two hundred guests had been invited and the caterers confirmed. She knew her timing was terrible. She had known it even as she drove toward the airport, but knowing had not stopped her.

"Keith, I just feel confused."

"Oh," he said with relief, "confused. Lacey, all brides have the prewedding jitters."

She didn't care if he was L.A.'s most persuasive lawyer. He wasn't going to convince her that a bride-to-be getting on an airplane and flying across a continent was nothing more than prewedding jitters.

"You've been doing too much," he said, his voice soothing, a man who had all the answers. For everybody. "My mother could have looked after wedding details. Or yours."

She felt petty for noticing his own services were not volunteered. He was probably right. The frantic pace, the dress fittings, the endless arrangements and appointments, the expectations coming at her from all sides that it was going to be *the* perfect fairy-tale wedding.

"Plus," he added, "you've been working in Divorce too long."

That was true. She'd seen more than her fair share of how those perfect fairy-tale weddings could end.

"Come on," he said. "Hop the next plane out of there. I can tell you're still at the airport. I can hear the luggage wheels rumbling by you. Come home. Everything's going to be fine."

She took a deep breath. Of course he was right. She was just suffering a terrible case of prenuptial jitters. Taken to the extreme by her close proximity to a Visa Gold card.

But then she suddenly caught sight of her own reflection in the glass around the cowboy. She looked very professional in her suit. Her blond hair was piled up on top of her head in a very corporate topknot. Well, her hair, being her hair, was falling out a bit on one side.

Still, she looked cool and calm and utterly professional, not at all like a woman who would ever lose her head or be irresponsible. Not like a woman capable of letting down her future groom, her parents, and two hundred confirmed guests.

She had the unnerving idea, studying her reflection, that it was like studying a stranger. That composed woman wasn't her at all.

"I've got to go."

"Calgary!" he said. "You're at the airport in Calgary. The number you're calling from has Calgary prefixes. If you won't come to me, I'll come to you. Grab a seat at the bar. I'll be there in—how long will it take me to get there?"

"Don't come."

"I'm coming," he announced.

She hung up the phone and began calling hotels. Only to find out even her Visa Gold wasn't going to buy her a hiding place in this town. Not tonight.

She sank into a chair and contemplated her options. She could fly somewhere else.

She realized she was being crazy, but a rebellious voice inside her head told her to go ahead and be crazy. Told her there was something wrong with being thirty years old and never having done one crazy or impulsive thing.

She had set goals and worked steadily toward them all her adult life. At eighteen she had started university. She had earned scholarships, maintained an A average throughout, passed the bar in the top percentile and nailed a job with one of L.A.'s top ten law firms. Not bad for a girl from a staunchly blue-collar neighborhood, a cop's daughter.

And now this. Her wedding, the final coup, the match made in heaven.

No one could have been more surprised than her when, driving back to work this afternoon, she'd been almost overwhelmed by a sense of— She forced herself to analyze it, sitting there in the airport. A sense of what?

Emptiness.

Emptiness, she chided herself. In a life so full she'd been unable to find time to have lunch for the past two and a half months? Emptiness?

Okay, piped up the recently released rebel inside her own brain, maybe *loss* would be a better word.

Loss.

But loss of what? She had everything. The career. The man. They were looking at a lovely house with a pool. A pool. Her father would be beside himself with glee if they bought it.

Get back on that plane, her responsible voice ordered her.

All right, she told it. But she did not move. She buried her face in her hands and allowed herself to feel totally exhausted. She couldn't even bring herself to go look at the front of the bronze statue.

She was a lawyer. She'd made it. She was going to marry Keith Wilcox, probably the most eligible bachelor in L.A.

Her parents were thrilled for her. Everybody's dreams for her were coming true.

Get back on the plane. She gathered up her purse. That was what she'd do. She could feel it now. The return of her senses. It had been madness, that was all. Just a few moments of utter madness brought on by too much divorce court, too much—

"Excuse me, ma'am?"

And Gumpy had stood there. And she had taken one look at him and let the madness come back, followed the light in his eyes toward an uncertain future.

And now she was here, lying in a lumpy bed, running her fingers through the hopeless tangles of her hair, hoping beyond hope some miracle would allow her to stay in this refuge for a while. To look after those adorable children, and to sort through her own confusion.

She decided, not for the first time, she absolutely hated her hair. And she decided, right before she slept, jockeys. He'd wear jockeys.

Wondering what the hell she was sleeping in kept Ethan awake until the dawn was touching the sky. He finally slept, awakening to bright light pouring in his window and the aroma of cooking food tickling his nostrils. Food that smelled like heaven.

It was the first time in two weeks he hadn't woken up with two little kids staring at him, their eyes only inches from his face. He was astonished to find he missed it.

He got up and dressed, hoping to catch Gumpy in the act of putting one over on him.

But it was Lacey McCade standing at the stove, looking dangerously at ease with a frying pan. Her hair was braided. She had on the same pink suit. It was impossibly rumpled.

He realized she'd slept in it.

"Morning," she said cheerfully.

He took a sip of the coffee she had handed him. Damn, it was good. Gumpy and the kids were already tucking into whatever was on their plates.

He was relieved to see it looked like slop.

"Omelette ranchero," she told him, setting a plate on the table for him as he sat down.

"Not too talkative this morning," Gumpy goaded him. "What do you think of the coffee?"

"It's okay."

Gumpy grinned.

A delicate smell wafted up to him—of eggs and onions and herbs. He bit into the omelette cautiously. Ambrosia. The slop was salsa. He glanced at Gumpy who was laughing at him.

She's not staying, he mouthed.

"Promises are important," Gumpy said out loud.

Ethan tried to think of exactly what he had said last night. It hadn't been a promise. Not even close. A bet. They hadn't even shaken on it.

Gumpy didn't believe in shaking. He believed in honor. If a man said something, he followed through. Even if he'd said it when he was dead tired and felt backed into the corner. Ethan realized he'd taken the bait—hook, line and sinker.

"So, how long could you stay?" Gumpy asked her, when Ethan failed to say anything.

She turned and looked at them, her face bright with hope.

Why would anybody even want to stay here? Ethan asked himself. A million miles from the nearest shopping mall with two kids who didn't obey, an old man and a grouch. Whatever she was running from must be pretty bad. A boyfriend who beat her? He inspected her visible skin areas for bruises, feeling some sort of unfathomable anger as he did so.

But he didn't see any bruises.

She was looking at him. He continued to eat his breakfast. He pretended to be engrossed in Danny's retelling of a dream about a monster who ate frogs and purple dogs.

"I could stay until you found somebody else," she said. "Two weeks tops."

Everybody was looking at him now. Danny was suddenly quiet.

Doreen laid her hand on his arm, leaving a little trail of salsa on the sleeve of his shirt, which was practically brand-new. "Oh, please, Unca," she said.

If he said no, she'd start crying. He just knew it.

And Gumpy, when insulted, sometimes went into the hills alone for days.

Which would leave him in an even more unworkable position than the one he had been in twenty-four hours ago. Ethan was finished breakfast, anyway. He scraped back his chair, and got up, went to the door and put on his hat and boots and coat. He waited until he had one foot out the door before he said, "Yeah. Okay. Whatever."

He didn't turn around to see Lacey McCade's reaction. He didn't want to see her reaction because he had the awful feeling that if she ever directed the full wattage of that dazzling smile at him, he would be lost.

Totally, completely, irrevocably lost.

He jammed his hat harder on his head and lengthened his stride.

Chapter Three

She was staying!

Lacey couldn't believe how elated she felt, how absolutely wonderful it felt to be a million miles from anything familiar. The view out the kitchen window this morning reminded her of that—a pastoral winter scene of barns, old fences, cattle and horses.

Now, as she paused for a moment from gathering the breakfast dishes to gaze again at the scene, Ethan came into her line of vision, walking down the road heading toward the barn. His hands were thrust deep into his pockets, his stride long and purposeful, his black cowboy hat pulled low over his brow. He kicked at an ice ball and it sailed down the drive ahead of him.

Clearly he was not sharing her elation. Not at all.

But Danny and Doreen were happy she was staying, sitting at the table telling her the one hundred and one things they had to show her.

Gumpy came and helped himself to a refill of coffee. "Thanks for breakfast." He glanced out the window, just in time to see Ethan send another ice ball sailing. "He'll come around."

"It's only for two weeks."

She put dishes in the sink and contemplated her timing. Two weeks. She could go home, cancel the wedding in plenty of time and do her best to put her life back together.

What was left of it.

If she went back, now, today, she could salvage something. It was a halfhearted thought. No, she'd said she would stay. She was needed here, whether the grump marching down the road wanted to admit he needed her or not.

And as for the grump... She was determined not to think about the grump. Or the amazing way she felt when he was in the room—not like an experienced trial lawyer, but like a high school senior with a crush on the school heartthrob. She'd nearly dropped his omelette right on his lap when his hand had inadvertently touched hers as she'd set it down in front of him.

If she stayed here too long, she might have to look at the deep throbbing within her that had started the very moment she had seen the cowboy snoozing on the couch. It was something between a pain and an ache. But nothing could happen in two weeks.

Meanwhile, she could help him out by giving him refuge from the niece and nephew who had so obviously wrapped that man of steel around their teeny-tiny pinkies. And he could help her out by giving her refuge from her life, just long enough for her to sort out what fierce instinct had broken through all her reserve and all her sense of responsibility and obligation, and *made* her get on that plane.

"Are we making cookies now?" Doreen demanded.

"Dishes first. Pull over some chairs, and you can both help me with them."

"Really?" they asked, wide-eyed.

Gumpy harrumphed with pleasure. "See you at lunch," he said, and then offered, "Something with meat in it might make him feel better."

She smiled. "Not according to the Heart Foundation, but I'll keep that in mind."

Danny and Doreen were still standing on chairs, meticulously wiping every drop of moisture off the plates, when Ethan came back in. Lacey had begun to do an inventory of supplies he had in his cupboards, making a list of items that would need to be picked up if she was going to do this job properly.

He'd hired her and she planned to make sure he got his money's worth. Plus, there was the little matter of proving to him that she was capable of a little more than matching her fingernail polish to the day's outfit.

He gave his boots a wipe at the door, then came into the kitchen with them on.

"That's okay, I haven't washed it yet," she said, looking out at him from behind an open cupboard door.

He scowled at her, the scowl of a man who was going to wear his boots in his house if he damn well pleased.

"Unca," Doreen said, and held up her plate for inspection. "Look-it. Me and Danny are helping."

He looked surprised, but he gave his niece's glossy hair a little ruffle with a big, leather-gloved hand. "That's great, sweetheart."

He turned away before he saw the beam of pure pleasure on the little girl's face. He opened the fridge, pulling a glove off with his teeth.

He retrieved a bottle of white liquid, and took off his

other glove, stuffing them both in the back pocket of his jeans.

Which was the only reason she even noticed the rear end of his jeans, she told herself. She looked for long enough to know jeans had been made for men built like him.

She watched as he slipped a huge syringe from his front shirt pocket, took the cap off with his teeth, shook the bottle, turned it upside down and inserted the needle, then pulled back the plunger.

"I hope that isn't for one of us," she kidded, amazed by his steady confidence with the needle and the bottle. From plumber to doctor in the blink of an eye.

He cast her a look. "Well, ma'am, I thought I heard you sneeze this morning." His face remained absolutely deadpan, but she saw the faintest glimmer of laughter in his eyes.

It changed him in the most remarkable way. For an astounding moment she felt she saw who he *really* was. A man with incredible depth, and a great capacity for life and laughter.

She ducked her head back into the cupboard, studying soup labels as if her life depended on it, listening to the kids hoot with delight.

"Lacey's getting a needle. Lacey's getting a needle."

"No, Lacey is not!" she said from behind the cupboard door.

She contemplated the way he had said "ma'am." Had he intended for it to come off his lips so slow and sexy, or was that just the cowboy way of saying things?

Thank God that smile had only flickered for a moment in his eyes, and had not touched his lips. If he ever smiled at her, she had the awful feeling she might be lost. Forever.

She slammed the cupboard door shut, jotted with furious efficiency on her growing grocery list and turned swiftly from him, not daring to look his way again. She went across the kitchen and opened the lid of the chest freezer, trying to concentrate on the contents and what they needed.

"Is Lacey getting a needle?" Danny demanded.

"No," Ethan said, putting the bottle back and closing the fridge door. "One of the cows is sick."

"Which one?" Doreen asked.

"I call her 131. I don't think you know her."

Shoving things around in the freezer until her fingers felt as if they might fall off, Lacy marveled at the patience in Ethan's deep voice.

"Is she brown?" Danny asked.

"Umm-hmm. Brown and white."

When Lacey had looked out the window, she noticed all the cattle were brown and white. Every single one of them.

"Is she big?" Doreen asked.

"Um-hmm."

They had all been big, too.

"Is she fat?" Danny asked.

"Just right."

"Is she going to die?" Doreen asked.

"Not if I can help it."

"Will she cry when you give her that great big needle?"

"She'll hardly feel it. I promise."

He was trying to escape twenty questions, moving toward the door.

"Is she—"

"Doreen, your uncle has work to do. You can save some questions to ask him at lunch."

She was suddenly aware of him. He had not gone out the door, but was standing behind her, and she whirled and looked at him. He was putting on a glove in a leisurely way.

"I'll get Gumpy to bring you in a couple of pairs of his jeans and shirts. Mine wouldn't fit you." His eyes moved down her in a lazy inventory. She was suddenly very sorry she'd been bending over the freezer like that.

She tugged down the hem of her skirt, then folded her arms across her chest.

"Speaking of questions, what made you take a ride with Gumpy?" he asked softly. "Didn't your mama ever warn you about strangers?"

He took a step closer to her. His eyes trailed over her hair, and fastened finally on her lips.

In the background, Danny and Doreen's chattering faded. The whole world seemed to become him. His cowboy hat, his broad shoulders under a faded sheepskin-lined jean jacket, strong, muscled denim-clad legs, booted feet.

Her whole world seemed to become his eyes. His lips.

His aroma. He was so close she could smell him, and he smelled wonderful. Of leather and animals and clean crisp air. No aftershave, just pure man.

Keith sometimes wore a Stetson which suddenly struck her as hilarious, and she laughed nervously and tried to back up, but her fanny was already against the freezer.

"My, my," he said silkily, "you're not afraid of me, are you? You seem like a big-city girl. You should know all about how dangerous it can be to go with a stranger."

He moved a step closer, dark amusement burning in his eyes as he looked down at her.

She tilted her chin up at him. "Are you *trying* to frighten me?"

He seemed to consider that. Her heart was beating a mile a minute and sped up some when those cool gray eyes fastened on her lips again.

He's going to kiss me, she thought.

It occurred to her she should be terrified.

But she wasn't.

At all.

In fact, she wondered, crazily, what his lips would taste like, feel like.

He leaned very close. "If I wanted to frighten you," he said softly—

She closed her eyes and held her breath.

"—all I'd have to do is open that door."

She opened her eyes and stared at him, and he tilted his head to indicate a door to her left. She glanced at the closed door and then back at him. He had stepped back. He tugged on the other glove.

"You still haven't answered my question," he reminded her. "Why did you come here? What are you running from?"

Of course he knew she was running from something. You didn't hop in a stranger's vehicle without so much as a change of clothes unless something was wrong.

"Some things in my life got very complicated. I needed to get away for a while. To think."

He was regarding her narrowly.

He was obviously a man who had never run away from anything in his entire life, but he nodded thoughtfully and she sensed he believed her. Reluctantly.

"A man," he said flatly.

"Partly." That surprised her, because it was true. It would be much easier if the problem was all Keith, but it wasn't—10 percent Keith, 90 percent Lacey.

"Did he beat you?" This was asked with a certain terse

casualness, but the fire that burned in his eyes made her stomach do the strangest swan dive.

Why would he care? He didn't even know her.

But he cared. Generically, she supposed. It offended his cowboy sense of honor.

"Of course he didn't beat me!"

"That's good." Very good for Keith, she sensed. "Where are you from?"

"Los Angeles."

Not a flicker of surprise in that handsome face, but he said, "That's a long way to run."

"Visa Gold," she said weakly.

"What do you do for work?"

"What makes you think I'm not a nanny?"

"Don't play with me."

She shivered. "I work for a law firm."

"You're just staying until I find somebody else. You wouldn't be staying that long if Gumpy wasn't so set on the idea." He turned away from her.

"Unca?" said Doreen.

"Yeah, sweetheart?" he said with one gloved hand on the doorknob.

"I really like Lacey. Don't you?"

"Yeah. Well. Whatever." He went out the door. It seemed as though he slammed the door a little harder than was necessary to shut it.

"I don't think Unca likes you," Doreen said, eyeing her with wide-eyed concern.

"I think maybe it just takes a while for your uncle to like people."

"Oh, no! He liked me and Danny right away."

It occurred to her that children saw people's hearts very clearly. They could see underneath the hard exterior, could see always what she had glimpsed briefly when that smile lit Ethan's eyes. One thing was for certain, Danny and Doreen were not the least bit intimidated by their scowling uncle.

"Maybe sometimes your uncle likes people right away and other times they kind of have to grow on him."

"Grow on him?" Danny asked with disbelief. "You're going to grow on him? How do you do that?"

"She lies down on top of him, and we cover them both up with dirt and then add water," Doreen told her brother officiously.

The lying down on top of him part painted a picture in her mind that made her mouth go dry and her cheeks grow hot. As if she knew anything about it. At age thirty, she often wondered if she was the world's oldest virgin.

It wasn't exactly the thing she wanted to make the *Guinness Book of Records* for.

"I meant he needs to get used to me," Lacey said.

"I think he just doesn't like pink," Doreen decided, eyeing her outfit critically.

"I think you're absolutely right," Lacey agreed. She tried to make herself stand where she was, but instead the rebel that had made her get on the airplane made her go down the steps of the landing and look out the window of the back door.

She was standing right in an icy puddle left from his boots, which served her right.

There was a horse out there, waiting patiently at the end of the walk, fully tacked. It had a black mane and tail and a brown coat that was thick and glossy as a beaver pelt.

Ethan was standing in front of it, his broad back to her. The horse was munching something, and she realized he had taken an apple out of the fridge for it. He must have stuck it in the pocket of his jacket. Because his hands were full? Or so that she wouldn't see?

And jump to the conclusion that a heart beat under that steely exterior.

He glanced back then, saw her in the window and froze.

For a moment they stared at each other.

Then he mounted the horse, whirled around and galloped off.

She didn't turn away until she couldn't see him anymore.

Seeing him on his horse spoke of his spirit. Free. Powerful. Tough. She sighed, feeling utterly foolish. Really, he wasn't any kind of romantic hero.

She could just imagine the look of horror that would cross his face if the word "romance" was even uttered in his presence.

She went up the stairs to the kitchen, determined to put him out of her mind. Determined.

"Are we making cookies *now?*"

"Yes. Right away. First I just have to—" Lacey took a deep breath and tested the knob of the door he had warned her about. Whatever was behind that door might be enough to scare her right out of his life. What could it be?

Half of her hoped the door would be locked, but it creaked open.

A skeleton?

A dead animal?

She peered in the door cautiously, and burst out laughing.

Untidy piles of laundry were scattered over the entire surface of the laundry room floor.

Ethan rode away from the house, knowing she was watching him, so foolishly cantering the horse on uncertain footing.

Well, it wasn't the first time a man had been foolish because a pretty woman was watching him.

But it usually wasn't him.

He'd taken this whole reclusive thing too far, he figured. Gumpy had been trying to tell him for years, now, he had to get off the ranch more, live a little.

But for the longest time this had felt like living. Not a little. A lot. Hard work. Fresh air. Horses. Cattle. This piece of land, this way of life, soothed something restless inside him that nothing else had ever soothed.

And, Lord, if he hadn't tried a lot of things and a lot of thrills. He'd flown pretty high on applause and ambition before he'd buried his best friend, then looked deep into his own soul and been dissatisfied with what he'd seen. He'd headed back to these hills.

He looked at other men now and did not understand their longings. Fast cars. Big money. Mansions. On this little patch of earth, Ethan already had everything he needed. And wanted, too.

Until last night.

And now he was aware of a deep and abiding hunger in himself, and deeply resentful of that awareness. Once a man felt something so raw, how did he ever make it go away again?

She'd thought he was going to kiss her in there.

He'd been aware of being relieved when she backed up against that freezer. Whatever she was, it wasn't a hooker.

She was too uncertain about her own appeal. Too—what was the word?

Innocent came to mind.

He rejected it. How could anybody be thirty years old and innocent in this day and age? From L.A. no less?

She was having problems with a man. She didn't have any ring on her finger, so he'd take her at her word. She needed a bit of time. He needed a hand.

She could scratch his back, and he'd scratch hers, which unfortunately conjured up a very disturbing mental picture in his head.

He ordered himself to stop. There would be no back scratching and absolutely no kisses, no matter how her wide eyes beckoned him, no matter how he longed to just feel the softness of her lips under his own. He would start making some phone calls this afternoon. She'd be out of here by the end of the week.

They were doing each other a favor. It wasn't as if he was going to marry her.

If you did marry her, a voice inside his head told him, a voice he was sure he had never heard before, *her name would be Lacey Black.*

Which conjured up an instant image of her in black lace. Which was worse than the back scratching image by a country mile.

"Hey," Gumpy said, coming out of the barn, "that colt's green as grass. What are you doing to his mouth?"

Ethan swore under his breath. "I was thinking of something else."

She was not, he decided, the kind of woman who would change her name even if she did get married.

"Like what?"

Ethan didn't answer, and Gumpy laughed. "Oh, that."

"Could you dig her up something to wear?" he asked coolly.

"Yessir, I could do that."

So by lunch, she was dressed in jeans and a plaid shirt,

and it should have been an improvement over the pink suit, but somehow her curves filled out those duds quite differently than Gumpy ever had.

Her hair was falling free of the stern braid, and curled around a face flushed from cooking.

Ethan was trying to keep his eyes on his plate, and off her backside, without much luck. The contents of his plate looked like that compost heap Gumpy insisted on keeping, and tasted like a little bit of paradise.

"Just beef stir-fry," she said, when he asked, placing wicked emphasis on the beef. And then she wrinkled her nose, which made her look closer to eighteen than thirty. "With frozen vegetables."

"It would taste better with fresh?" he asked with disbelief. Maybe he shouldn't be in such a sure-fired hurry to get rid of her. This lady could cook. He glanced at the jeans again. Obviously blue jeans had been designed with her in mind. She had to go. It didn't matter if she could cook.

"Are you kids minding Lacey?" he asked gruffly. It was the first time he had said her name out loud. He tried very hard not to think of anything lacy.

Doreen and Danny both regarded him solemnly and silently, which he took for a no. But Lacey did not look worn down by them. Not at all.

Doreen, having his attention, put her fingers in her milk and splashed.

"Stop it," he said, and sighed when her eyes filled up with tears. "In Rotanbonga," he felt compelled to tell Lacey, "the people don't believe in disciplining children. They just kind of run wild until they're eight or something. My sister felt it showed respect for their culture to raise her own children according to their custom."

"It's always good to respect the customs of other people,'' Gumpy said, but he cast a rather doubtful look at the children who were both splashing in their milk now.

Lacey got up and removed both glasses of milk from the table, and then sat back down as if nothing had happened. "Could you pass the soy sauce?" she asked him pleasantly.

He glanced at his niece and nephew out of the corner of his eye. He was pretty sure they were doing the telepathic thing and would start screaming in unison. Instead, as he picked up the bottle of soy sauce, they both quietly returned to eating.

He met Lacey's gaze with surprise, and then noticed how the flannel shirt hugged the fullness of her breasts and opened on the creamy white of her throat. If he could have tossed her the soy sauce, he would have, but he passed it to her, and his hand brushed hers as she took it. He nearly dropped the damned stuff in the middle of the table.

It didn't really matter if she was good with the kids, either. She was disruptive.

Gumpy, though, didn't seem to be of the same mind. He took an appreciative bite of his meal and sighed. "You don't always get what you want," he said sagely. "But you get what you need."

"That's a lovely statement," Lacey told him sincerely. "Is it part of your native philosophy?"

Ethan snorted.

Gumpy looked sheepish.

"What?" she demanded.

"Rolling Stones," Ethan informed her.

She laughed. It chased some worried shadow from her face. It made her look vibrant and alive. And happy.

She absolutely had to go.

"I gotta go make some calls," Ethan said, getting up

from the table and ignoring Gumpy who was now humming the Stones' tune with enthusiasm. He grabbed a handful of cookies off the heaping plate on the counter on his way out the door.

He paused for a moment and listened. If he was not mistaken, the washer was thumping into a new cycle.

He went into the little cubbyhole that passed as his office and shut the door behind him. He found the phone under a leaning stack of papers.

He studied a cookie with interest as he dialed the number of his next-door neighbor. Maybe she had another cousin like Mrs. Bishop.

The cookie looked a bit like a bear dropping.

Cautiously he bit into it. And closed his eyes in pleasure.

He was on his sixth call, and his seventh cookie, when a soft knock came on the door. "Come in."

She came in. "Any luck?"

His office suddenly seemed very small. She smelled like a tantalizing combination of cookies, spices, soap and woman.

He shook his head. "I think the word's kind of out around here."

"What word?"

"About child-rearing philosophies in Rotanbonga."

"They're really just normal little kids."

"If that was normal, no one would have kids. No one."

She smiled wryly. "The people in Rotanbonga seem to still be having them."

He supposed the powerful pull of the male-female dynamic was responsible for that. He was certainly feeling that pull right now.

A man looked at lips like hers and thought one thought.

And the natural consequence of acting on that thought did not even enter his mind.

"I can only stay two weeks," she told him. Was she looking at his lips, too? Thank God she could only stay two weeks. Nothing could happen in two weeks. Except maybe she could make a hell of a dent in that laundry.

"I'll have found someone before that," he said with a confidence he was not feeling.

"The kids are just giving you a run for your money. Doreen has figured out the big tough cowboy is scared to death of a few tears, so she turns on the waterworks at every opportunity."

He stared at her. Doreen, a five-year-old, was manipulating him? Successfully? If he couldn't even outwit a five-year-old member of the female gender, he didn't have a hope with one his own age. Which was why he lived way out here. He instinctively knew it.

"You seem awfully good with them," he admitted reluctantly.

"I love kids. I wanted to be a schoolteacher, once upon a time."

She was thirty years old. If she loved kids that much, why didn't she have some? The question seemed a bit too personal, so instead he asked, "What happened?"

"Oh." She looked uncomfortable. "It was just something I thought of for a while."

Maybe, he thought, she didn't have the brains for it. Though with every passing minute with her, he became uncomfortably aware she was a hell of a lot smarter than he had first thought.

"We're going to need a few groceries." She was changing the subject, steering it deliberately away from her personal life. She presented him with a list.

He looked at it. He didn't even know what cumin was,

unless you counted the way the guys at the rodeo talked. He had a disturbing mental picture of himself wandering through the grocery store with a bewildered look on his face, having to ask some teenage girl where the cumin was, and he pushed the list back at her.

"Can you drive a truck?"

"Just like a car?" she said hopefully.

He nodded. "Except for the standard transmission."

"Oh. Standard transmission."

He could tell a standard transmission to her was what cumin was to him. He sighed.

"Sorry," she said.

"It's okay. Mrs. Bishop didn't do standard, either." Why was he trying to make her feel better?

"How urgently do we need stuff?"

"You have a freezer full of meat. And not much else."

"Meat's fine."

"I'm also desperately in need of a few items of clothing Gumpy couldn't supply."

He glanced at her sharply and was amazed to see she was blushing slightly, and even more amazed to feel the heat in his own cheeks.

"I'll take you to town this afternoon."

"Thank you." She turned away.

"Great cookies, Lacey."

She turned back and gave him a pleased smile.

Her teeth were white and straight, and her eyes sparkled.

He had known her smile would be lethal. Known it. He picked up the phone and dialed with renewed fervor. The door closed quietly behind her.

The phone buzzed busy, and he realized he had dialed his own number. A little shakily, he also realized that life as he had known it was over.

Chapter Four

Ethan played country music on the truck radio and looked straight ahead.

The truck was large, a crew cab with a flatbed on the back. Danny and Doreen were in the back seat, quietly looking through the books Lacey had unearthed for them out of a small stack of unpacked boxes in their bedroom.

After a few minutes Ethan glanced back at them, astonishment in his expression. "They're usually arguing by now," he commented as he pulled out of his driveway onto the gravel road.

The countryside was breathtaking to Lacey. They were in the foothills of the Rocky Mountains, and she marveled to herself at the space, and the wildness of it, and the lack of population. It was very clear to her that he belonged in this land. That it would demand strength and ruggedness and that Ethan Black had both. And some to spare.

They turned off the gravel onto the blacktop. They passed a green sign that named the distance to towns,

Priddis, Millarville, Turner Valley, Sheep River, Black Diamond. Ethan glanced again at the back seat. "They're usually fighting by now."

Lacey glanced back at the twins. Their shiny heads were bowed over their books. She reached back and ruffled one and then the other, and they looked up at her with heart-melting smiles. It seemed to her they had managed to win her affections, totally, in a shockingly short amount of time.

There was a song on the radio that might have been about Ethan.

About a lonely cowboy, stubborn, strong and untamed, running from the temptations of his own heart.

"I usually have to stop right here," he said, nodding toward another sign, "and pull them apart." He cast her a look. "You didn't drug them, did you?"

He was teasing, but she couldn't tell, save for the smallest twinkle that briefly warmed the slate-gray of his eyes and the slight tilt upward in the stern line of his mouth.

The truck suddenly seemed too closed in. She could smell him, and the aroma was absolutely heady. Intoxicating. He had showered when he'd come in from his ranch work, and now he smelled of soap and shampoo and other things tantalizingly and completely male.

Though she, too, was trying to look straight ahead, out of the corner of her eye she kept catching glimpses of his strong forearms as he steered the truck.

On the radio the song had reached a point where the cowboy had to surrender to the girl or ride away into the sunset.

For a moment she had the awful feeling that instead of Ethan's ranch offering her refuge, she had walked smack-dab into danger of a sort she had never faced before, and only understood slightly. She waited to see how the song would end, as if it might provide a clue to the mysteries of her own heart, but Ethan reached out and snapped off the radio impatiently.

"Why did you do that?" she asked.

"I'm listening to the engine. Hear that little clicking noise?"

She listened, but heard nothing but the hum of a perfectly healthy-sounding engine. But then, what did she know? Engines, plumbing—they were all equally baffling to her. A fact she suspected he was counting on so he wouldn't have to explain why he'd really turned off the song.

She'd be willing to bet it had something to do with mushy endings.

They passed through several tiny, rural hamlets before Ethan finally slowed on the outskirts of a small town. To Lacey the town of Sheep River looked charming and quaint and old-fashioned.

Ethan pulled into a parking stall. Doreen and Danny set down their books and were craning their necks like small turkeys trying to see out the window.

"Are we here?" Doreen asked. "Oh, goody."

"We better make a plan," Ethan said grimly.

"A plan?"

Doreen and Danny undid their seat belts. They began jumping up and down on the back seat with excitement.

"Last time I did this, I got in that store and Doreen went one way and Danny went the other. There are no grocery stores in Rotanbonga, or at least none that they had ever been in."

"We love stores!" Danny announced to Lacey loudly.

"Remember what I told you?" Ethan asked, twisting

in his seat and fixing the twins with a look that would have made just about anybody quiver in their boots.

There was silence, except for the steady thump of the twins jumping up and down.

"Last time," he told Lacey in an undertone, "they went wild."

"How wild?" Lacey asked, also in an undertone.

"I found Doreen in aisle seven chowing down on as many different kinds of cookies as she could cram in her mouth. Danny was gift wrapping aisle three. In toilet paper."

The grim expression on Ethan's face warned her that absolutely the wrong thing to do would be to laugh. Lacey laughed.

"It really wasn't very funny," he informed her sternly.

"Of course not. No." She tried to stifle the laughter. It slipped out anyway. She looked out her window, her shoulders shaking.

"You're going to find out," he promised her.

She took a deep breath, bit the side of her cheek and looked back at him solemnly. "I'm sure we'll manage."

"Yes, we will. Because I have a plan."

"Which is?" She wouldn't have been surprised if he rolled out a reconnaissance map of the grocery store.

"I'll take Danny to the machinery shop with me. I need a part for my tractor—"

"No-o-o!" Danny howled, still hopping. "I want to go in the store!"

Ethan looked perplexed. "Okay. I'll take Doreen and—"

"No-o-o!" Doreen howled, still hopping. "I want to go with Lacey."

"I'll stay in the truck with them," he decided, a true leader, adapting his plan to the changing requirements of the mission, "and go for my tractor part after you get back with the groceries."

Danny and Doreen screamed "no" together.

"Ethan," Lacey said gently. She laid her hand on his sleeve. "Go get your tractor part. The kids and I will go shopping."

"Yes!" they shrieked in approval.

Ethan stared down at his sleeve. She became aware of the warmth that radiated from his arm, the utter strength there, the yearning that leaped to life in her soul. Oh, what it must be like to touch the silk of his skin and the steel of his muscles. She hastily yanked her hand away.

She was not a woman given to passions. Cool. Calm. Collected. That was Lacey McCade. You didn't abandon one man one day and feel this way about another one the next. You simply didn't.

Okay. She did. She had felt it. There was no denying that. But feeling and acting on a feeling were two entirely different things. It was just a bizarre form of stress. Possibly a way of trying to escape the real question, which was what she was going to do about her messed-up life.

Her real life.

"You don't know what you are letting yourself in for," Ethan warned her.

"Danny and Doreen," Lacey said, "stop hopping and listen to me for a second before we go into the store."

She had Ethan's undivided, if cynical, attention. The twins froze in place.

"This is a store," she told them. "We have to buy things from the store. All the items on the shelves have to be paid for. They are not free and they do not belong to us until we have paid for them. Do you understand that?"

The twins nodded solemnly in unison. Ethan rolled his eyes.

"This is a food store, not a toy store. You are not allowed to play with anything in the store. Do you understand that?"

Again they nodded. Ethan sighed loudly. He might as well have said out loud, *Such naiveté*.

"I have never been in this store," Lacey continued, "and so I will need your help finding things. You must not leave me or I could get lost."

Solemn nods.

Ethan groaned.

"Each of you may choose one thing that is not on my grocery list. It must be something healthy. Not candy or potato chips or ice cream. No junk."

The nods were eager this time, except for Ethan who said under his breath, "No ice cream?"

"No junk," Doreen and Danny agreed solemnly.

"This is not going to work," Ethan warned her.

"I bet it does."

"I don't think I'm taking any more bets today. Doreen and Danny?"

They looked at him, anxious to please.

"I don't want the sheriff coming to get me from the tractor store, understand?"

They looked baffled, but they nodded anyway.

"I have an account in there," he told Lacey. "Just put anything you buy on the account. I'll meet you back here at the truck."

He opened his door, got out and pulled down the brim of his cowboy hat. He muttered, "No ice cream?" under his breath once more and then walked across the street.

Lordy, he was an easy man to look at. She watched him, marveling at the power in his long stride, the easy confidence in the set of his shoulders. It was only after he was out of sight that she gathered up Doreen and Danny.

With their hands snugly in hers, it occurred to her that the world had rarely felt so real.

Lacey took the kids into the store. They were wonderful. They really never had been in a grocery store before their last visit to this one, and Lacey delighted in seeing such ordinary things through their fresh young eyes. They were brimming with curiosity and asked a million questions, but they behaved beautifully, anxiously debating their choices at each aisle as Lacey picked out the other items they needed.

Finally, Doreen chose bacon.

Danny chose small single-serving yogurts for him and his sister.

Lacey chose chocolate ripple ice cream. For Ethan.

She double-checked her list, then brought the heaping grocery cart, Doreen and Danny now riding shotgun on the sides of it, to the checkout.

There was only one checkout open. The girl working there looked very young, perhaps sixteen or seventeen. She had her pretty brown hair pulled back into a tight ponytail, and she wore a huge name tag that said Alice on it.

"Would you put this on Ethan Black's account?" Lacey requested, showing the twins how to unload the items onto the conveyor belt. She was used to the anonymity of the big city, but knew Ethan's life had just gotten harder when Alice gawked at her and stammered, "Ethan's?"

"I'm his nanny," Lacey tried to explain. Through the big picture window at the front of the store, she saw

Ethan come out of the tractor shop across the street with a bulky parcel.

"He needs a nanny?" the girl choked.

"The children," Lacey said pointedly. Doreen and Danny smiled at Alice.

"They look just like him!" Alice exclaimed.

Lacey headed off the rumor at the pass. "Evidently you weren't here last week. This is Doreen and Danny, Ethan's niece and nephew. They're visiting him for a while."

She could see Ethan at his truck, anchoring his big parcel to the flatbed.

"Oh. His niece and nephew," Alice said with mingled disappointment and relief.

Disappointment that such a potent rumor had been nixed before it began, and relief that the area's most eligible bachelor was still eligible? Lacey could only guess.

Ethan came through the door at that moment, and Lacey saw a look come onto Alice's face that confirmed at least part of her guess. That look more normally would have been reserved for a rock star or movie idol.

Actually, Lacey understood it better than she wanted to. With his long legs and broad shoulders and that cowboy hat pulled low over his eyes, Ethan looked like the quintessential cowboy, the ultimate romantic hero.

And she couldn't think of a role he would be more uncomfortable playing.

"Hi, Ethan," Alice said breathlessly. "Ridden any bulls lately?"

The girl was cute as a button, and Lacey waited to see Ethan's response, even as she tucked away that fact. Ridden bulls?

"I'm looking at bulls from a different angle these days," he said mildly.

"Unca," Doreen shouted. "I picked bacon."

She ran up to him, and he picked her up with easy and unselfconscious strength, kissed her on the tip of her nose and set her back down. Then he blushed.

"I picked little yogurts for Doreen and me, and I was a really good boy. Wasn't I?"

"Of course you were, Danny. You were wonderful, too, Doreen."

Ethan looked disgruntled. He picked up several bags of groceries.

Alice said, "I can give you a hand with those."

"No, thanks." His tone was perfectly flat. If there was no interest in it, there was certainly no judgment of her silly offer, either. He pushed open the door with his big shoulder, and an icy blast of air came in before the door slapped shut behind him.

Lacey selected a small bag for Doreen to carry out, and one for Danny. She picked up the remaining bags. Alice did not offer to assist her.

"I wish I would have known he was looking for a nanny," Alice said wistfully, watching Ethan through the big glass window as he put things in his truck.

In all fairness Lacey could tell her the position would be open in two weeks. But her tongue seemed to be glued to the roof of her mouth. She went out the door, followed Ethan's example and put the groceries in a large plastic box strapped to the back of the flatbed.

"Those other things I needed?" she asked him.

He took a sudden interest in arranging a bag of groceries. "Try over there." He nodded to a store across the street. His ears were a cute shade of red.

"Will you be okay with the kids for a few minutes?" He looked doubtful, but he nodded proudly.

The store was a small dry goods emporium that stocked

a limited selection of jeans and work shirts, wool socks and plain white underwear. They even had nail polish remover. After she had quickly selected all the items she would need to get through a couple of weeks, Lacey couldn't resist adding miniature denim overalls and plaid shirts for each of the twins. At the cash register, the clerk, an old man in overalls, stared at Lacey's American money with bewildered horror. When he took a worn pencil from behind his ear and began to do calculations for the exchange rate, she handed him her credit card, which he accepted gratefully.

She got back to the truck to find Ethan standing outside it, his arms crossed over his chest and his cowboy hat tilted over his eyes. There was an unholy racket coming from within the vehicle.

"They're fighting over who gets the red yogurt and who gets the blue one."

It was one thing to feel these flare-ups of passion for him. Something so primal could be easily tamed. But the small stab of tenderness she felt at this big, rugged man's helplessness in the face of these two adorable waifs was something else altogether.

"Ethan," she told him, mildly exasperated, "you need a crash course in kid control."

She thought he might tell her what he needed was a real nanny. Or thirty-four hours in a day instead of twenty-four. Or two tickets to Rotanbonga.

Instead, he grinned. It made him look ten years younger, and wildly handsome.

"I've got everything I need," he told her, tapping his front pocket.

She looked at him quizzically.

He pulled up the little box in his pocket. Earplugs.

She shook her head, laughed and got in the truck. She

told the kids they could each have half of each of the small containers of yogurt.

He climbed in, tinkered with his box of earplugs for a moment, and then suddenly realized the twins were silent. "How did you do that?"

"Negotiations," she murmured. "My specialty."

"Do you think yogurt was a healthy thing to pick, Unca?" Danny asked him.

"Sure, Danny, right up there with bean sprouts."

Danny beamed.

"And what about bacon?" Doreen demanded.

"I was a little worried about the bacon," Lacey confessed under her breath. "All that fat. Not to mention the nitrates."

"Nitrates," Ethan echoed, sending a look over his shoulder to his now-quiet niece and nephew. "I don't care if you knock the pork industry," he decided, flicking the ignition on. "I don't raise pigs."

"That girl in the grocery store seemed quite taken with you," Lacey said casually, looking out the side window of the truck.

"Did she?"

"She said she wouldn't mind being your nanny."

"You didn't tell her I needed one, did you?" he asked, shooting a glance her way.

"Would it matter?"

"I don't need another kid to baby-sit."

Lacey liked it that he wasn't even a little flattered by the pretty young girl's attention.

"What did she mean about riding bulls lately?"

He hesitated. "I used to ride. A long time ago. Way before her time. I'm surprised she even knew about it, but this is a small place. She may have heard some grossly exaggerated tale of my short career."

"It was your career?"

"Pro rodeo. For a while."

"Were you in the Calgary Stampede?"

"Once."

"When I was young, I always wanted to go to a rodeo."

"Why?"

"I'm not even sure. It was a stage I went through as a girl. Why did you ride bulls?"

"It was a stage I went through as a boy." There was something grim in his voice.

They had almost had a conversation, she realized, but the No Trespassing signs were up in his voice now. So she was surprised when, after a few miles had gone by, he spoke again.

"So you never went to a rodeo?" he asked. "Ever?"

"I saw a few on TV."

"What did you like about it?"

The way those bold young men looked in their blue jeans.

"It was exciting," she said. "It was the most unpredictable thing I'd ever seen."

She decided not to tell him that at one time it had seemed like the most wildly romantic thing she had ever seen, those seemingly fearless young men pitting themselves against huge menacing bulls and twisting, wild-eyed horses. She understood perfectly why Alice had looked at Ethan the way she had.

And she understood something else.

That urge she had followed yesterday to do something unpredictable had not been as new and foreign to her personality as she wanted to believe.

Doreen started shrieking at Danny.

Ethan put his earplugs in.

It was a mistake, Ethan thought as he unpacked groceries, to make her laugh.

Her laughter had a lovely sound to it, but it was what it did to her face that was dangerous. It was as if a light went on in her eyes, chasing some ever-present worry away.

He watched, surreptitiously, as she put all the groceries away, and felt something else dangerous budding within him.

It would probably be a fairly easy thing to fight off a fleeting attraction to a laugh. He'd fought off lots of fleeting attractions.

But respecting her. That was something else. And how could he not respect her? She was no nanny, and yet she had taken to the twins like a duck to water.

He'd underestimated her. He knew that. She was no empty-headed beauty.

When he saw her unpack the chocolate ripple ice cream, he felt a flash of irritation just like the one he'd felt when he'd turned off that song on the radio on the way to town. That stupid song that ended with a perfectly good range rider riding herd on a baby of his own.

She could be smart and efficient if she wanted.

But she'd better not make him feel anything. Like the way he'd felt earlier when she laid her hand on his sleeve in the truck, and told him she could manage those kids by herself.

For a moment, he'd felt...not alone, he realized.

He snorted at himself. As if he was alone. He had Gumpy. He had the twins.

Yet it wasn't the same as her soft touch on his sleeve. Not even close. That had been something more than not being alone.

Tenderness.

The word shocked him. He was not sure he had ever activated it in his vocabulary before.

"Lacey, I'll take the kids down for a ride while you get dinner ready," he heard himself saying.

There was a plan. Get away from her. Her shining hair. Her soft curves pressed into the unfamiliar fabric of her new shirt. Her smile.

Especially that smile.

But take the kids? Now why had he gone and done that? The idea wasn't to make this job easier for her. It was to get rid of her.

Of course, he had to find somebody else first.

And it wasn't going to be Alice Dempsey. Not if his life depended on it. She was too spinny, though she wasn't nearly as young as she looked. She always regarded him with those annoying stars in her eyes.

He'd like to take her aside and say to her, "Kid, there is nothing romantic about a cowboy. They're stubborn and set in their ways, and self-centered as all get-out. You go find yourself a nice lawyer or accountant or something."

There had been a song that said it all. A Willie Nelson tune. He should send it to her. Anonymously.

So for somebody stubborn and self-centered, why had he offered to take the kids off Lacey's hands? The truth was that he liked the kids.

Okay, they were bad as far as kids went. They didn't obey, and they broke things and flushed things down the toilet and they had darn near wrecked the grocery store when he had taken them there last week.

But still, they filled some part of him with—damn it, there was that word again—*tenderness*.

"Unca's teaching us to ride," Doreen said proudly.

"That's wonderful," Lacey said, and she smiled at him. "I always wanted to learn to ride."

He got the kids ready, jamming them into jackets and boots and mittens and wool hats, and contemplated Lacey's comment.

It seemed to him that she had an awful lot of things she had always wanted to do, and had never done.

She probably made it up.

Why would she have ever wanted to ride?

But later she appeared at the fence, wrapped in an old jacket of his, watching with a wistful look on her face as he got Doreen to walk old Chief around the arena.

"Look at me, Lacey," Doreen called. "Look at me. I'm doing it all by myself."

"I'm next," Danny announced. "I'm going to trot today. Chief's a big horse, not a pony."

"I can see that," she said to Danny. "Chief's beautiful," she called to Ethan.

Chief was a big hammer-headed part Appaloosa with pink around his eyes and muzzle. You would have had to look hard to find an uglier horse.

The wind was biting, and she didn't appear to be dressed for it, and yet she stood there with a rapt look on her face as Doreen and then Danny trotted the huge old gelding around the arena.

Don't ask her, Ethan warned himself.

"You want to try it?" he asked her.

She looked astonished. "Me?"

"You're the one who always wanted to learn to ride," he reminded her.

"Oh, I know, but—"

"Come on."

She hesitated, and then a big smile lit her face and she ducked through the fence.

He changed saddles, aware of her watching him with interest.

"Could I try that? Please?"

"What?"

"What you just did?"

He had tightened the cinch, but he untightened it and stepped back. He watched with amazement as she duplicated his knot exactly. Not that it was complicated, it was just that most people took a few tries to catch on to things.

Over the smell of leather, and Chief, he could smell her.

"Get on, Lacey," Danny shouted encouragingly.

She was very close to Ethan. Her hair had fallen nearly completely out of that braid.

He decided he hated this.

"Put your foot in the stirrup. That's it." He prayed he wasn't going to have to touch her. To give her a push on her delectable little fanny to get her into the saddle.

She managed by herself, in quite a graceful and athletic manner.

He found himself feeling slightly resentful of answered prayers.

Her whole face was radiant as he gave her a few simple instructions how to guide the horse around the corral. Then he watched her move off. She threw back her head and laughed out loud.

"This is wonderful," she called. "Wonderful."

She rode around the corral clockwise and then he switched her to counterclockwise. She had nice balance, and sat the horse sweetly.

After twice around the corral, she stopped in front of him, slipped off the horse, and handed him the reins, regret in every line of her face. "I think I'm burning supper."

For a moment he debated telling her to let it burn. The joy in her face was so radiant. But he knew that might be moving onto dangerous ground, so he took the horse's reins and watched her run lightly up the hill toward the house.

When they walked into the house after finishing up the chores, it smelled wonderful.

Gumpy was already there, sitting at the table, chatting with Lacey as though they had been lifelong friends.

"She's making us chicken jumbo-somethin' or other. Jamaican," Gumpy informed him with pleasure.

The aroma made Ethan feel as if he was going to float. He took the twins down the hall to the bathroom and scrubbed off their hands, and then his own.

When he got back, the chicken jumbo-something was on a platter on the center of the table in a bed of rice.

Frankly, it looked like hell.

But he was no longer so easily fooled.

It was excellent.

"Where the hell is this in my cookbooks?" he asked, not sure that he could go through life without having it again.

"You shouldn't use *hell*," Doreen told him. "My daddy says *H-E-double hockey sticks* instead, and we all know what he means."

"Good for your daddy," Ethan said. "Which cookbook is this in?"

Lacey smiled. "I didn't realize you had cookbooks."

Gumpy sighed happily, but Ethan eyed his gorgeous intruder warily. He couldn't exactly think of a polite way to ask her if she'd had a cookbook up her dress when she'd arrived.

"I remember things," she answered him before he asked.

Again he felt a small fissure of warning. She was no blond bimbo. Weren't recipes kind of exact things? A teaspoon of this, and a pinch of that? How could anyone remember them?

She made sundaes for dessert. Chocolate ripple ice cream, with whipping cream and chocolate sauce.

"This is about as close to heaven as a man gets in this lifetime," Gumpy proclaimed.

Ethan agreed, not that he was about to say so out loud. He got up from the table and went to his office and shut the door.

He had a nanny to find. Just about anyone but Alice would do. He began to make phone calls. He could hear the twins laughing as they helped with the dishes, and later as they splashed around in the bathtub.

Then the house was quiet. He emerged from his office, and was disappointed to see the twins were already in bed. They had gone to sleep without him saying goodnight to them.

In the living room, Gumpy and Lacey were playing cards.

"I'm teaching her to play poker," Gumpy said. "You in?"

Of course he wasn't in. He had a ranch to run. He had a night's sleep to catch up on. He had a nanny to find.

"No," he said from the doorway, more sharply than he intended.

Gumpy shrugged and dealt the cards. He knew some of the world's most ridiculous poker games. For "Blind Baseball," they each got four cards down which they got to look at, but the fifth one they had to hold up on their forehead, so they couldn't see it, but their opponents could.

Lacey was nearly hysterical with laughter. It seemed to Ethan it had been a very long time since anyone had laughed that way in this house.

After she went and checked on the kids, Gumpy looked at the little pile of toothpicks in front of her place and shook his head.

"She's going to own my tepee soon."

"Beginner's luck."

"I don't think so. She remembers the cards that have been played."

Ethan looked at Gumpy. He willed himself back to work. If he was going to stand in the doorway all night and watch them play cards, he might as well have joined them.

But he did not want to think about joining the circle of their warmth and laughter.

Lacey came back, and she and Gumpy resumed play, a more-typical hand of five-card stud. Ethan watched her closely. Gumpy was right. She was remembering the cards that had been played.

"What did you say you did in that law firm you work for?" he asked casually.

"Did I say?" she hedged.

"You want to come to Las Vegas with me?" Gumpy asked her. "You have a photographic memory, don't you?"

She shrugged. "I guess it could be called that."

Ethan pressed. "What do you do for that law firm?"

She showed her hand. "I'm a lawyer."

He closed his eyes. Not very long ago he'd told himself he'd go for brains in a woman before beauty.

And now he had a beautiful, brainy woman sitting in

his living room. She could play poker. And she could cook. She loved kids.

But, he reminded himself desperately, she was a lawyer. A career woman. The novelty of the ranch and the twins and her first horseback ride and poker hand would only take her so far. Besides, she was on the run from something.

And so was he. He'd realized it just this very second. His own damn fool heart.

Chapter Five

Lacey lay in bed, reviewing her first four days on the ranch. She had learned to play poker. She had ridden a real live horse. She had seen a snowfall. She had tobogganed. She had baked enough cookies to feed an army.

When she had leaned over to kiss Doreen good-night tonight, the child's small, surprisingly strong arms had twined around her neck and pulled her close.

"I love you," Doreen had whispered.

It was silly, really, to feel as wonderful as she did inside.

She had accomplished so much in her life. And none of it had ever made her feel so good as the extraordinarily simple events of the past several days.

Of course, if she was really honest with herself, she was pretty sure that the excitement that unfurled in her stomach like a gently waving flag didn't have very much to do with baking cookies, or making sure the whites got white.

Perhaps not even that much to do with discovering the pure joy of riding a horse or flying down a hill on a sled.

It was him...

She felt such a strong pull toward Ethan. Something in the set of his features stirred a deep and mysterious longing within her to know him. Nothing more than that, of course. She still had a whole life waiting to be sorted out a million miles away.

Still, whimsically, she wondered if the pull of him had reached across a continent, called her soul, pulled her toward that off-ramp that day. As long as he remained remote, she was relatively safe.

Except that even when he was remote, he still showed her who he was in the way he deferred to Gumpy with such quiet respect, in the way he would toss the twins in the air until they were howling with delight and in the way his eyes would rest on his niece and nephew, the gray suddenly warmed with unguarded tenderness.

Still, there had been no further invitations to horseback ride.

In fact, she was fairly certain he was avoiding her.

Mornings he got up very early, looked after himself and was out of the house before another soul had stirred. Once, she had heard him and stumbled out of her room at six in the morning to find him in the kitchen making instant porridge with hot water from the tap! He took more time on the coffee he left ready for her.

The next morning she had been determined he was not going to put in a hard day's work with a stomachful of porridge made with tap water. She had set her alarm for five-thirty. But she'd woken to find the coffee ready and him gone, and realized it was useless. If she got up at five-thirty he would get up at five, and he had a streak of stubbornness in him so strong that before she knew it they would be getting up at midnight trying to beat each other to the kitchen.

Three out of four days he had come in for lunch. He ate quickly, chatted with the twins, discussed ranch business with Gumpy, always thanked her politely for her efforts, and was gone again. Something about his voice would linger with her all afternoon.

He was always in for dinner, but three out of four nights he had grabbed a plate, teased the twins for a few minutes, thanked her and then taken his dinner to his office.

"He likes you," Gumpy announced with satisfaction, hearing the office door slam behind Ethan.

Lacey had rolled her eyes, but now, lying in bed, she contemplated that. Maybe it wasn't as absurd as it seemed. If Ethan did not feel the same pull as her, why was he going to such great lengths to get out of her way?

She should be thanking him, really. Her life was quite complicated enough.

The problem was, she did not seem to be using her time here to sort out the complications of her life, to ponder the situation between her and Keith, to come up with solutions. She had spoken to her father, very briefly yesterday, on the phone. She knew he didn't have call display.

She had been driven by guilt to call him, thinking he would be worried about her. Her father had a bad heart. She didn't want to cause him worry.

He had been outraged. The wedding had been canceled. He'd ordered her home as if she was three, and not thirty.

"You better figure things out, little missy," he'd yelled before she hung up.

Figure things out. That was precisely why she was

here. Her thoughts should have been on where she would go from here, what the future held.

But they weren't. Her thoughts seemed to be consumed by living moment-to-moment. Playing with the twins. Reading to them. Helping them make crafts. Cooking. Keeping up with the laundry. Playing poker with Gumpy.

Restless, Lacey got out of bed. The house was dark and silent, and she padded quietly down to the kitchen. She went into the laundry room and took a load out of the washer and put it in the dryer.

There was a small window in the laundry room, and she looked out it, noticing the night was bright. A white circle of a full moon hung over the ranch, and had painted the world outside the window ghostly silver and gray. There was a grove of thick trees this side of the house, and she had not explored it yet in her ventures with the children. Rather, time and again, it seemed, she'd been pulled toward the corrals in hope of catching a glimpse of Ethan at work.

She gasped suddenly, and squinted through the tangled branches of the trees.

There was a tepee back there! A full-size tepee, nearly hidden among the trees.

And then she gasped again when the laundry room light was turned on and she was bathed in its fluorescent glare. She was wearing one of the men's flannel shirts she had bought, and her legs were bare.

Ethan stood there in jeans and bare feet, his chest as naked as her legs. Something flashed in his eyes, white-hot, and then was quickly hooded.

"Sorry, I didn't mean to startle you. Danny walks in his sleep from time to time. I seem to sleep with one eye open, wondering if he'll head outside."

She tried to compose herself, to still the wild beating

of her heart. The man's chest was magnificent, deep and sculptured. Focus on what he's saying, she ordered herself.

"Danny sleepwalks? Could we get something for the doors? Put a lock high up?" Her eyes drifted from his chest to the chiseled flatness of his stomach.

"I'll put one up tomorrow, as long as you promise to unlock it before Gumpy comes in the morning. He'd break down the door if anything kept him from his coffee."

His arms were smooth and corded with muscle. His skin was the most beautiful copper color.

"You're the first one out the door," she reminded him. She forced herself to quit acting like an infatuated teenager, to prove he had no hold over her. She turned back to the window.

"I guess I am." His voice was low and husky, as sensuous as a touch. "Lacey, I don't pay you enough to be doing laundry at midnight."

She laughed shakily and used all her willpower not to look back at him, to drink in the pure beauty of skin, of his molded muscles, of his naked chest, with the raw thirst of one who had wandered too long in the desert.

"I was just up, anyway. I couldn't sleep."

"Is everything all right?"

She closed her eyes against the unexpected concern in his voice, a voice that was like a touch of velvet against a soft cheek.

"Fine," she said. "It couldn't be better. I just noticed there's a tepee out there."

Ethan came and stood beside her. "That's where Gumpy lives."

He smelled of soap and of leather and wood smoke

and horses and other things so masculine it made her mouth go dry.

"Gumpy lives out there? In this weather?" she asked, trying not to make it too obvious how deeply she was inhaling his scent.

"That's what I said to him. In this weather? You try and talk him out of it."

"Has he always lived like that?"

Ethan was standing much too close to her. Out of the corner of her eye, she could see moonlight playing across the surface of his skin. She longed to touch him. She cupped her hands primly in front of her.

"No, he started a year or two ago."

"I was going to have some hot milk. Did you want something?" She brushed by him, the laundry room suddenly entirely too small for the two of them.

She knew he would say no. He would thank her politely and go back to bed. Thank God.

"Not hot milk," he said, and made her feel about as exciting as a little old lady with a dozen or so cats. "Maybe I'll have some more ice cream."

Her heart began to pound. She and Ethan were going to spend time together. Alone. She suddenly did not feel at all like a sophisticated lawyer from L.A. She felt like a tongue-tied teenager. She went to the freezer, but he took her shoulders and put her gently out of the way.

"I'll get it. I don't like you working night and day."

"I wouldn't know what to do with myself without eighty billable hours per week. Not that I'm billing you by the hour." There, she had reminded herself who she really was. If her shoulders were not tingling where his hands had gripped them so briefly, she might even believe it.

"Thank God. I doubt if I could afford you. Do you like being a lawyer?"

He heaped a bowl with ice cream and sat down at the table. She deliberately turned from him and poured her milk into a saucepan.

It was a simple enough question. She wondered why she had never asked it of herself. "It's okay," she said. "Why does Gumpy live out there?"

Far better to turn the conversation away from herself and away from the puzzling restlessness of her own spirit than to start examining things too closely.

"About three years ago he was at a friend's house, and they showed *Dances with Wolves*. He'd never seen it before. I hadn't, either, to be honest. The next day he bought a VCR and the movie."

Lacey remembered seeing both items under the TV set.

"I'd love to see it again," she said.

Ethan groaned. "Please don't tell him that."

"Why?"

"We've watched it at least eighty times. He knows all the words. For a while he called me Dumb-Bear. I told him I wanted to be Wind in His Hair, but he said he was going to be Wind in His Hair. That was about a two-week argument."

Lacey couldn't help but smile at the thought of those two bachelors watching that movie over and over again, arguing about who was more suited to which roles in it.

"I told him he should be Ten Bears, but no, it had to be Wind in His Hair." Ethan became serious. "He said that movie righted many wrongs that had been done to the People. He said it made him proud of his heritage. Then one day he announced he was going back to the old ways, and he started working on the tepee. About a year later he moved in. He still likes a few modern conveniences. The shower. The coffeemaker. The blender.''

"He's a remarkable man," Lacey said with real affection. She poured her hot milk into a cup and joined him at the table.

"I know," Ethan said. "You should go see him out there sometime. It's incredible inside. Heaped up with pelts and skins and furs. He makes bows and tans hides and does beadwork. He loves company, but you have to take him a gift if you go."

"A gift?"

"To show your respect for him as an elder. It used to be tobacco, but he doesn't smoke. I usually bring him a candy bar, or a tin of cocoa. Something like that."

"You go see him often," she guessed.

"Oh, sure. Before the twins came, if we weren't watching *Dances with Wolves,* I'd go out there. He tells me things. My mother is a Sarcee Indian. Tsuu-T'ina. He tells me about her people. My people. He shows me the old ways."

Lacey could tell this meant a lot to him just by the way he was trying to make it seem like it didn't. "What kind of old ways?"

"He shows me how to make things. Drums. Pipes. Bows. Arrows. Arrowheads."

"That's wonderful."

"It passes time on a long winter night," Ethan said with a shrug.

But suddenly she could see him, bent intently over the drum or the bow, firelight flickering off his face, the blood of his ancestors so much a part of who he was today. "You're proud of your heritage, too," she guessed softly.

He looked surprised. "I guess I am, though I don't

really know when that happened. When I was in the first grade, some little kid called me a dirty Indian and I came out swinging. That sort of set the pace for the rest of my life. I always had something to prove.''

''What happened?'' To Lacey, it seemed as if she had never met a man who seemed to have less to prove. He was a man without the stuff, the BMW, the mansion, the career.

And yet when she looked at Ethan, he seemed to have everything he needed. A deep sense of himself. Dignity. A connection with the earth and animals. Strength. He seemed to be a man who knew how to be true to himself and his own spirit.

And in a sudden moment of clarity she wondered if that was not why she was here. To learn those same things. ''What happened?'' she asked him again, more urgently.

''Gumpy as much as anything.''

Gumpy. Somehow she was not surprised that her airport angel had something to do with Ethan's quiet confidence. ''How did you meet him?''

''He just showed up one day, looking for a job. I had just taken over the ranch. My parents retired to Arizona. He works for me, but you probably noticed I'm not the boss.''

She laughed. ''The twins seem to be the boss.''

This time he laughed.

She would have given everything she had to make that moment last between them, but he was already getting up. He rinsed his dish in the sink. It wasn't a big thing, but it was not something Keith would have ever done.

''Good night,'' he said. He turned from the sink and looked at her.

For a moment everything within her went still. All the

force and energy of her will begged him to cross the room, to gather her in the strength of his arms, to kiss her senseless.

"Good night," she stammered.

He stood a moment longer, as if caught in the power of her mind calling him, and then he turned and was gone.

The milk grew cold in front of her.

Ethan went back to his room and shut the door firmly behind him. His heart was pounding in his chest.

She obviously had no idea how lovely she looked in that too-large men's shirt she had worn to bed, her long legs bare, her hair down and tangled around the perfection of her face.

It was everything he had been able to do to stop himself from stampeding across the room and taking her in his arms, and taking her. Tasting her with his lips, touching her with his hands. The desire he felt was white-hot within him, and it was not cooling because he had come to the sanctuary of his bedroom and closed the door.

He'd been doing so well. Getting up earlier than her in the mornings and getting out the door before she was even up. Okay, he had to miss those glorious breakfasts she cooked, but it was a small price to pay not to have her crowding around in his mind all day.

Not that he was kidding himself.

She was crowding his mind, even though he didn't have breakfast with her. Even though he ate quick lunches with her and shut himself in his office with his supper.

He was trying to avoid her because he knew.

A man was not made of steel. Not this man. He knew the embers of the fire were within him, waiting for the smallest breath of air to leap to life, flaming and out of control.

He'd been doing so well at avoiding her. But he missed the twins.

Then tonight, seeing her in her nightshirt in the laundry room, he'd known to just go right back to bed.

Instead, like a fool, he'd had to test himself. Watch her sipping milk right across the table from him, listen to her soft voice and rich laughter. Felt her calling to some place inside himself that he had been blissfully unaware existed.

It had been a long time since he had sat across the table from someone and felt so comfortable. So content.

Gumpy didn't count.

But that very comfort, that contentment, had been the breath of air the fire needed. He listened to her bedroom door close. He listened to the squeak of springs as she climbed into bed. He felt sweat pop out on his brow, shoved his hands deep in his pockets, and went to his window.

He wondered, now that he'd seen her lovely legs bare, if every time he looked at her he was going to feel distracted.

His window faced Gumpy's tepee. He noticed a light flickering within it.

Did that old man ever sleep?

He pulled an old sweater over his chest and put on some socks. Leaning beside the dresser was the bow he was working on, and he picked it up. Quietly he let himself out his door and went back to the kitchen.

She had baked brownies today, and he had refused them as if they were laced with her potent brand of magic.

He took one now and popped the whole thing in his mouth. He'd been right to deprive himself. They were laced with magic, rich and creamy and absolutely delicious. He carefully wrapped two in plastic to take to Gumpy.

He didn't bother with a jacket, just put on his boots and went out the back door. He went up the well-travelled trail into the thick grove of trees that surrounded the lodge.

Gumpy told him to come in before he even got to the door flap.

Ethan ducked through the opening and felt himself transported back through time. It was warm in the tepee and smelled richly of smoke, both from the fire that burned at the center pit and from the cured hides.

Gumpy sat cross-legged on a heap of buffalo hides, looking at the fire, wearing a beautiful shirt of tanned leather.

He looked almost as though he were expecting company at one o'clock in the morning, Ethan thought. Silently he passed him the bow and the brownies.

Gumpy set the brownies carefully at his feet and then inspected the bow at length and in silence. Finally he gestured for Ethan to sit.

Gumpy set the bow down and said simply, "You honor the Creator with this work."

Ethan waited to see if Gumpy would invite him to speak, but he didn't, and in a way Ethan was glad. His confusion was very personal. It was not quite the same as when he had first sat with Gumpy, his heart still aching over the death of his best friend, Bryan Portland. At that time two years had passed since Bryan had died and yet Ethan's pain had seemed as fresh as the day Bryan had been gored to death by a bull at a rodeo.

There had been no tepee then, not yet. No *Dances with Wolves*, either. But Gumpy had been a healer even then.

Ethan was not even sure how the old man had worked his particular brand of magic, only that he had and that his own journey to his true self had begun.

His heart had a funny ache in it now, too. But as he sat in silence, in the flickering golden light of the fire, it occurred to him that it was a different kind of ache altogether. Not about death this time, but about life. About choices. He allowed his confusion about the woman to roll through his mind.

After a long time Gumpy looked away from the fire and directly into Ethan's eyes.

He said, "The Creator gives a man all he needs for joy. But He does not make him accept it."

Ethan glared at Gumpy. Was he talking about her?

Gumpy apparently decided not to enlighten him further. With a sigh of happiness he ate both his brownies, tugged off his moccasins, pulled off his beautiful shirt and crawled under his buffalo hide. Within moments his soft snoring filled the tepee.

Ethan got up and went outside. It was a beautiful night, the moon full and bright, the stars brilliant in the sky. The air was cold and crisp and clean.

Everything he needed for joy, Ethan thought dubiously.

"Get to know her," Gumpy's muffled voice came from inside the tepee. "What could it hurt?"

Hurt. Now there was an interesting word.

Bryan had been his best friend since first grade. When he'd been slugging that other kid for calling him names, suddenly Bryan had been at his side, slugging away, too. They'd laughed and slugged their way through adolescence. They'd learned to ride the bulls together. They'd discovered the mysteries of girls together. He knew what Bryan was thinking before he said it.

They'd both been hurt, and hurt plenty, riding bulls.

But Ethan hadn't known the meaning of the word *pain* until Bryan was killed.

It occurred to him he had not really cared about anyone since. Not in a deep way. Not in a way where he could be hurt like that again.

But then along came Gumpy. And then the twins. And now her.

What could it hurt?

The answer was *plenty*. It could hurt plenty.

He didn't even know who she was. The little bit he did know did not point to her staying around here. Or having the time of day to give a cowboy.

He thought of her looking at him across the space of the kitchen only a few hours earlier, her eyes liquid, beckoning him, calling him.

He could be in over his head before he knew what had hit him.

But did he really want to go through life never taking a risk because he'd been hurt once?

At least when he rode a bull, he thought cynically, he wore a vest that protected his chest, his heart.

He didn't think they made that kind of equipment for other kinds of heartaches.

Of course, he could ask Gumpy, the self-proclaimed expert on everything.

Lacey was astounded the next morning when she got up and went into the kitchen. Ethan always made the coffee before he went out, but today he was still at the kitchen table, looking over some papers. He was wearing a plaid flannel shirt, but now that she knew how he looked underneath that shirt, she wondered how she was ever going to look at him again without feeling distracted.

Gumpy was there, too, sipping coffee and looking

faintly smug, though not a word passed between the two men.

The twins got up and came into the kitchen looking rumpled and sleepy, just as she was cutting quiche and putting it on the table.

She took her seat. "Gumpy, all the time I've been here, I had no idea you lived in a tepee. I saw it out the laundry room window last night. It looks beautiful."

"Oh, it is," Doreen said. "It's beautiful. Unca takes us there and we sit around the fire on animals that are rugs now. Gumpy tells good stories about the coyote. He's the Trickster. That means he plays tricks on people."

"My grandma is a Sarcee Indian," Danny said proudly. "She's in Arizona with Grandpa right now. Unca Ethan, you should show Lacey her dress."

"Unca Ethan" nodded but didn't look up from his breakfast or the papers he was looking at.

Then he looked up suddenly and glared at Gumpy, and Lacey had the feeling Gumpy had kicked him under the table. Hard.

Ethan cleared his throat. "Lacey, if you want to bring the kids down to the corral around four, I'll give them another riding lesson." He winced, and she thought he might have been kicked again. "And you, too," he said in a low voice.

"I'd love that," she said, and it was true, even if he had been coerced.

Gumpy looked very pleased. Ethan did not.

What could it hurt, she thought, to get to know him? Just a little bit before she had to go?

Later, as they walked down to the corrals, Doreen confided her Uncle Ethan was her favorite person in the whole world, right after her mommy and daddy.

"I think I'll marry him when I grow up," she decided.

Danny glared at her, obviously seeing this as an unfair advantage. "Then I'll marry Lacey!" he decided.

Lacey laughed. "Doreen, little girls don't marry their uncles. Besides he's much too old for you. And I'm too old for you, Danny. I'll be forty-five years old by the time you're ready to marry anyone."

"That is very old," Danny decided. "But I'll still love you."

"I'll still love you, too," she whispered. "I promise."

The twins would grow up without her. She would never know about all the wonderful little events of their lives. Or the big ones, either. How they liked their first-grade teacher, if they were going back to Rotanbonga.

How could that possibly hurt so much? She had only known them five days. She ordered herself to quit being so sentimental. She could write letters. She could use the phone.

Ethan was waiting at the corral with Chief, and she watched him with the children. He really was wonderful with them, very gentle and patient. Watching him look up at Doreen as she sat in the saddle, explaining something to her about what to do with her hands, she knew that she would never write. Or phone.

That she would never look back.

"Just enjoy the moment."

She started. Gumpy had materialized at her side, and somehow read her mind.

"You're getting a furrow right here," he said, rubbing above the bridge of his nose. "You worry too much."

She smiled. "I suppose I do."

"You should come see me sometime. At my lodge."

"I will."

Gumpy watched the riding lesson, his dark eyes alight

with pleasure as he watched Doreen and then Danny. When the children were done, he surprised her by telling them he would take them up to the house for hot chocolate while Ethan gave Lacey her lesson.

As they walked away, Lacey heard Doreen tell Gumpy she was going to marry him when she was old enough.

"I'm too old for you," he said.

"Oh, Gumpy," Doreen said incredulously, "you'll never be old."

Danny, obviously angry that Doreen kept playing the marriage card, gave his sister a shove. Gumpy separated them and took each by the hand.

Lacey knew he did not feel any more comfortable with small children than Ethan did, so his offer both touched her and raised her suspicions.

Was Gumpy matchmaking? Lacey blushed at the thought.

Ethan busied himself changing saddles.

He was all business as she mounted the horse. He made her walk the horse around the corral, then reverse directions. He moved her up to a trot, and she hung on for dear life as the big horse jogged around, rattling her teeth. But finally, she was able to get her mind off what Ethan's chest looked like under that jacket and shirt long enough to hear what he was saying, and the trot became less bone jarring as she adjusted her weight in the saddle.

There was something about controlling the big horse that made Lacey feel wonderful.

"Lacey, you want to try him at a lope?"

"A lope? Like running?"

"A slow run. It's easier to sit than a trot."

Suddenly she wanted nothing more. She nodded, and he told her how to set up for it, how to nudge the horse out with her heels and use the reins.

With her heart beating in her throat, she walked Chief up the length of the corral, turned him and trotted toward Ethan.

Then, she pushed Chief one step further. She felt as if she was flying. The wind tugged at her hair and touched her face. The horse felt so strong beneath her, and she felt as if she was being allowed to be part of his power.

She felt utterly, wonderfully, absolutely free.

She went by Ethan and followed the corral fence around in a circle. With each stride the horse took, she felt more natural on his back, felt more strongly the sense of delight and freedom.

It wasn't until she stopped that she realized she was crying.

She never cried. Hardly ever. She had been a successful woman in a man's world too long. Somehow even the tears felt like freedom.

Ethan strolled toward her, and she wiped at the tears, but not soon enough.

His mouth dropped open, and he ran the last few steps. "Lacey? What's the matter?" He pulled her down off the saddle and into the circle of his arms. "Are you hurt? What happened?"

"I'm not hurt," she said, knowing she should pull away from him, but unwilling. "I don't know why I'm crying. It's silly. I guess I just never felt anything quite so wonderful."

Except what she was feeling right now. His arms around her, pressed so close to him that she could feel his heartbeat matching her own.

"You're okay, then?" The relief in his voice, the unguarded caring, made something in her sing.

He put her away from him and scanned her face. He

took a leather-gloved hand and wiped a tear from her cheek. He looked astonished.

"It's just a horse," he said gruffly.

"For you, it's just a horse. For me, it's a childhood dream come true. Could I do it again? Please?"

He nodded, and she remounted the horse.

And she rode and rode and rode. She rode until the sun had faded from the sky. She rode until her hands were numb with cold and her nose felt as if it was going to fall off.

And even though she shouted at him that he did not have to stay to watch, he sat on the fence and watched her.

And she was so glad that somehow he was a part of that moment when everything changed for her.

When, for the first time in her life, she felt free.

Chapter Six

"Lacey, you laugh a lot," Danny told her approvingly.

"I do?" Lacey had always been the serious one. But now it seemed to her that she had been given a gift from the heavens. And she had eight days left to enjoy it. The gift was this: to live life to the fullest.

And she did. She played in the snow. She baked cookies with happy faces made out of smarties. She enjoyed the twins. She laughed until her stomach hurt at their crazy antics.

Yesterday, when she had come in from her ride with Ethan, that exhilarating ride that had filled her soul until it nearly ran over with joy, she had come into the house to find Gumpy's entire head swathed in toilet paper. Only his mouth showed, and the twins were spooning mysterious dark liquid into that.

"We're medical missionaries," Doreen announced. "We fixed Gumpy's head, and now we're giving him medicine."

"Medicine?" Lacey had asked with alarm. "What kind of medicine?"

"Maple syrup," Gumpy's muffled voice had said.

Lacey had thought she would die laughing. She had been the next patient, and she had cheerfully fallen to the floor, moaning loudly about her leg.

Broken, the resident medical missionaries had diagnosed, though luckily they had their cure-all right there. With deadly serious efficiency Dr. Doreen and Dr. Danny wound toilet paper around her leg while she groaned loudly.

Ethan had come in and stared at the scene, shaken his head and gone to wash up for supper. But before he had turned, Lacey knew she had seen laughter touch his eyes.

And after supper he surprised them all by allowing himself to be docilely led off to be the next patient. Lacey did the dishes and listened as Doreen ordered his socks off.

"Your toes hurt, don't they?" she diagnosed.

"Yes, ma'am," he played along. "They sure do."

"Fractured," Danny announced.

One of them must have touched one, and Ethan howled with pretended pain. Doreen and Danny laughed and touched his toe again, and he howled again, a mournful bay.

Gumpy joined Lacey at the sink and took a dish towel and began drying the dishes. He and Lacey exchanged a look as Ethan howled, and Danny and Doreen screamed with laughter as the howls grew in volume and length.

Gumpy smiled to himself, a deeply contented smile, and said, "You go horseback riding again tomorrow. I'll look after them."

Lacey thought only briefly of protesting.

Another gift. And she accepted it gladly.

Now, still feeling warmed from Danny's remark about her laughing a lot, she put the last touches on the peppercorn mustard sauce and poured it over the beef. She popped it in the oven just as Gumpy came in.

"This has to be turned down in an hour, all right?"

"Turned down in an hour," he repeated dutifully.

"Gumpy," Danny called, "come in the living room. Today we're going to be the policeman and guess what you get to be?"

"The bad guy?" Gumpy guessed.

"Yes," the twins squealed.

"Are you sure you're going to be all right?" Lacey asked.

He rolled his eyes.

Dressed in a warm winter jacket of Ethan's, and with a wool hat, gloves and a scarf on, she ran down to the corral. When she got there, Chief was already saddled. And so was the bay colt she had seen Ethan ride the first day.

"Are you feeling ready to get out of the corral?" Ethan asked her gruffly, flicking her a look over his shoulder as he tightened the girth on his saddle.

She was scared to death, actually. Out of the corral? Beyond the limits of safety? No fences?

But a gift was a gift, and she knew better than to pass on this opportunity. She had to take what life offered with both hands. Was this not why she had taken the exit ramp? Because life had become altogether too safe? Too dull? Because living had become a chore, instead of an adventure?

"I'm ready," she said.

He rewarded her with a small smile that tilted up at one corner of his mouth.

She watched him mount his horse, the foot in the stirrup, the easy swing up.

She decided to imitate him exactly, but somewhere it went wrong, and she ended up sprawled across the saddle on her tummy, her legs wagging behind her. With a terrible grunt of exertion she finally managed to get into the saddle.

She glanced at Ethan.

The small smile had become a grin, boyish and endearing.

"Don't make fun," she warned him sternly, gathering up her reins.

"Why? What would you do to me?"

"Sue you." She adjusted her feet carefully in the stirrups.

He laughed. His laughter was deep, right from his belly. It lit his face, and his spirit danced in his eyes.

She looked at him and knew being able to see him like this was part of the gift.

"You'd have to catch me first, lawyer lady."

It was a challenge if she had ever heard one. He spun the horse away from her and galloped to the corral gate.

She hesitated for only a second and then plunged her heels into Chief's sides, startling the horse out of his sleep. He took a plodding step or two forward, and then at her insistence broke into a reluctant trot.

Meanwhile, Ethan had stopped and opened the corral gate without getting off his horse.

He glanced back at her and had the audacity to stick out his tongue before he galloped across the snow-covered pasture, puffs of powdery snow flying up at his horse's feet.

She hesitated. What if it was slippery?

She could feel her forehead crease and willed it not to.

She could almost hear Gumpy telling her she worried too much, and she decided not to. Not for eight more days, anyway.

She was ready. For whatever life threw at her.

Chief broke into a smooth, slow lope. She had no hope of closing the distance between her and Ethan, but she felt it again. That sensation of utter freedom. Of joy. Her hat blew off and her hair scattered around her face. She laughed out loud.

He must have checked his horse, because she did gain on him, until she was right behind him, and then Chief pulled out beside the other horse, and they were loping through the snow side by side.

They came to the end of the open field, and the horses slowed and then walked. She reached out playfully and tapped Ethan's broad shoulder.

"Tag," she said. "You're it."

You're it. The words rang in her head. It. The one. The man she could give her whole heart and soul to.

She paled at the thought. Because she was not the kind of woman Ethan would ever go for. He'd want someone every bit as strong and self-reliant as he was. A woman who could fix the plumbing and wrangle the horses right along with him. A woman who cooked plain old roast beef. No mustard-peppercorn sauce.

It wasn't that he was it, anyway, she rationalized desperately. It was not even about him. It was about the feeling inside of her. He just happened to be there when it got let out.

They took a trail that twisted through the timber, going up and up and up.

Finally they were at the top of a stony ridge, the horses blowing warm clouds into icy air.

Ethan swung off his horse. "You want to get off for a minute? Give your legs a stretch?"

Her legs nearly buckled when she got off the horse, but Ethan was at her side in an instant to steady her.

He brushed her hair back off her face. "Where's your hat?"

"I lost it back there."

"Are your ears freezing?"

"Why would they be?" she asked proudly. Her ears actually felt as if they had fallen off some time ago. "Your ears aren't covered, and they're not cold."

"That's because I'm tough as old hides. Besides, I get used to the cold weather coming gradually. You're taking, what, a seventy-degree drop?"

"Well, they're not cold," she said with stupid pride.

He pulled his gloves off his hands, and reached over and covered her ears.

"They feel a touch cold," he said with a smile.

His hands felt beautiful on her ears, radiating heat. She closed her eyes blissfully. "My hands are a little cold, too," she said.

After a minute he took his hands off her ears and unraveled the scarf from around her neck, and tied it snugly over her head.

She scowled at him, thinking she probably looked about as attractive as a wrinkled old grandma in her babushka. But then he slipped her gloves off and held her cold hands between the warmth of his.

"Mitts are better," he told her, "but they're hard to ride in."

Mitts are better, he'd said in a calm voice, her hand in his obviously not doing any of the things to his heart that it was doing to hers. The sudden flare of heat in her belly radiated outward and her hands warmed almost instantly. He let them go and turned and regarded the view.

"Put your gloves back on," he ordered absently.

"And if I don't?"

He grinned at her. "I'll sue you."

They stood side by side gazing down at the Sheep River and the valley below them. His house looked like a little dollhouse with smoke pouring out the chimney, the outbuildings scattered around it, the Rocky Mountains looming up behind it.

Gifts from heaven? She was in heaven.

"Sometimes," he said softly, after standing silent and unmoving for a very long time, "I stand here, and I wonder if one of my ancestors ever stood on this point and looked out over this land before it was tamed. I think how wild and beautiful it must have been, and how wild and beautiful he must have been, and I feel connected to everything. To history and the earth and myself."

He had let his guard down. He had showed her a bit of who he was, a tiny glimpse of his soul.

You're it, that voice inside her, that terrible little voice that would not be tamed, told her silently.

"We better go," he said. "You're shaking."

And she dared not tell him it had nothing to do with the cold, but with a savage war being fought inside herself.

An hour later, the horses looked after, they opened the door of his house to the smell of something burning.

Without taking off his boots, Ethan raced up the stairs and across the kitchen. He threw open the oven door, and a cloud of black burped out.

He took the pan and tossed it in the sink. He peered at the contents.

"Roast beef," he decided sadly.

Lacey stared at the disaster and then listened with trepidation to the silence. She went into the living room. Gumpy was in the big wing chair, arms and legs bound with colorful bandannas. He was snoozing contentedly. The twins were side by side on the couch, fast asleep.

Ethan came up behind her. She could feel his breath on her neck. She wanted to lean into him. She wanted him to touch her shoulder.

He said, "You go have a nice hot bath. I'll fix something for dinner."

They ate peanut butter sandwiches for supper. Doreen and Danny announced it was their favorite ever.

"Unca Ethan," Doreen cried, "let's show Lacey Grandma's dress. Please?"

Ethan seemed to hesitate. "Okay," he agreed.

Except for Gumpy, who was worn out from his afternoon as a criminal, and who left right after supper, they all filed down the steps into the basement. The basement was full of boxes, and the single bulb threw eerie shadows. It didn't seem to perturb the twins who darted in and out of the maze of boxes until they came to a lovely, old stand-up wardrobe.

The twins threw open the door, and Ethan reached in. The dress was hung with a slender, stripped tree branch running through the sleeves.

The twins oohed together.

Lacey felt her eyes filling with those ridiculous tears again.

The dress was absolutely beautiful.

It was the softest leather, very light-colored, almost white, with beautiful fringes at the sleeves and the hem, and beadwork across the bodice.

"It's the most gorgeous dress I've ever seen," she

breathed, and her hand reached out of its own volition to touch it. The leather was soft as velvet and smelled beautiful, of leather and smoke. "Where on earth did it come from?"

"My grandmother made it for my mother for her wedding," Ethan said. Lacey cast him a quick look. Was there some sadness in his voice?

The twins were rummaging through a box they had found in the bottom of the wardrobe.

"Here's Grandma and Grandpa's wedding," Danny said, holding up a picture. "But Grandma isn't wearing that dress."

Lacey took the old photo. Ethan's mother was tall and willowy with gorgeous hair that flowed black and silky to her waist. Her beautiful eyes were very gentle. But she was not wearing the dress. In fact, she was wearing a very traditional wedding gown.

Ethan's father was a big man, strong looking, his eyes so like Ethan's it was like a mirror image. The look in his eyes as he gazed down at his bride was one of obvious adoration.

Had Ethan ever looked at anyone like that? Would he ever?

"Why didn't she wear the dress?" she stammered.

Ethan came and looked over her shoulder, then took the picture from her.

"It wasn't fashionable to be Native American back then."

"Oh, Ethan!"

"She wanted my dad to be proud of her. She wanted to fit into his world."

"Did she ever wear it?"

He nodded. "My sister and her husband brought the

twins home for their third birthday. They christened them at the same time. My mother wore it then.''

''She said she would never wear it again, though,'' Doreen said.

''What?'' Ethan said with obvious surprise.

''She said it's for your bridle, Unca Ethan. I didn't understand what a bridle was then, but I do now. It's the thing to steer the horse. Why does it need a dress?''

''I think she must have meant it was for Ethan's bride,'' Lacey suggested, feeling the strangest surge of emotion when she thought of a woman marrying Ethan in this dress.

Was the emotion envy? It felt even deeper. Like sorrow.

''What's a bride?'' Danny asked.

''It's the woman your uncle is going to marry,'' Lacey choked out.

Doreen's eyes got very round. ''I didn't know you were going to get married, Unca Ethan. When Lacey told me you couldn't marry me, I thought that was it for you.''

Ethan seemed to be studying the construction of the wardrobe box.

Lacey squatted down and sifted through the box of old photos. She came across a baby picture of Ethan. He was unmistakable. Black hair sticking out like cat fur, fat cheeks, a scowl.

''Are you getting married?'' Doreen demanded of her uncle.

''No!'' His reply had a very strangled sound to it.

''Are you getting married, Lacey?'' Danny asked.

Next week that was exactly what she would have been doing.

''No!'' she answered, her voice as strangled as Ethan's had been.

Doreen regarded them both for a moment. "You could marry each other!"

"Ohh," Danny breathed.

Lacey dared not look up. She studied a picture of Ethan, about age six, mounted on a full-size brown-and-white horse. His baby fat was already gone. His face was solemn. He already looked surprisingly in control of the world.

"Could you marry each other?" Doreen asked. "Please?"

"Doreen," her uncle said firmly. "That's enough. Go and play."

Doreen regarded her uncle solemnly for a moment and then she and Danny found some empty boxes and soon they were crawling in and out of them.

Lacey smiled to herself. Ethan was actually getting it. That as long as he meant it when he said something to the kids, they would do exactly as he asked.

There was another boy in many of the photographs. He was very blond, and a reckless light danced in his eyes and in the impish upturn of his mouth.

"Who is this?" Lacey asked.

Ethan took the picture from her. "Bryan Portland. He lived on the neighboring ranch."

"You were good friends," Lacey said, looking at a picture of the two of them wrestling on the lawn in front of this very house. The tree in the front yard had grown about twenty feet since the photo had been taken.

"The best."

"Are you still?"

There was a long silence.

"He died," Ethan finally said, levelly. "He was killed by a bull."

Lacey scanned Ethan's face. Though she sensed he was

keeping his features deliberately bland, she saw the pain in his eyes.

"I'm so sorry. Doing ranch work?"

Ethan shook his head. "At a rodeo."

She remembered the day they had driven to the store and Ethan had asked her, so grimly, what she liked about rodeos. She was sorry she'd ever been attracted to a sport so brutal it killed people. "I'm so sorry," she said. "You were there, weren't you?"

"I was. He died in my arms on the way to the hospital."

He leaned over and took the picture from her hand, put it back in the box and fastened the lid. He put the whole box back in the wardrobe with his mother's dress and shut the door.

"I should have stopped him from riding that day," he said.

She scanned his face, and could see immediately that he was annoyed at himself that he had not succeeded in closing the subject by closing the box. Annoyed at himself for telling her.

"Why?" she asked softly. "Why should you have stopped him?"

"He wasn't feeling good. You can't make mistakes riding bulls. You have to be 100 percent there, and he wasn't. He'd been drinking the night before."

"And could you have stopped him?" she asked gently.

Ethan seemed to think about that. "No. I don't think I could have."

She sensed now was not the time to probe deeper. She turned from him. "Come on, Danny and Doreen. Bath time."

When she turned back, Ethan had already gone up the stairs.

After the twins were in bed, the house seemed empty and quiet. She could hear Ethan behind the door of his office, on the phone, talking to one of his neighbors about a nanny.

"Old," he was saying. "A roast-beef-and-potatoes kind."

She went to the back porch and got a jacket. It was time to pay Gumpy a visit. At the last minute she remembered she needed to bring him a gift.

She had made gingerbread with the kids that morning. She had made a gingerbread horse and decorated his rump with spots. She wrapped him and slid him into the pocket of the jacket.

She stopped awkwardly outside the tepee. "Hello," she called.

"Come."

She unfastened the flap and pulled it back, ducked to get through and then refastened it from the inside.

She turned and took a deep and awed breath.

Gumpy's lodge was as beautiful as she had been led to believe.

Gumpy himself looked different. He was wearing a leather shirt that reminded her of the dress she had just seen.

He looked grave and dignified and very, very wise.

Somehow not like the Gumpy she had come to know at all.

He gestured expansively for her to sit down. First, she passed him the gingerbread horse, and his look of childish pleasure made him her Gumpy again. Then she crossed her legs and dropped into the heavy buffalo wool beside him.

"It's wonderful in here," she said, looking into the leaping flames of the fire, loving the way the light played off his work and his face. "I love your shirt. Did you make it?"

"From buckskin. Brain tanned, according to the old way."

"Brain tanned? Does that mean——" she gulped "——you used brains?"

He nodded with pleasure. "I get the brains from the slaughterhouse. Then I put them in the blender——"

"The blender? In the kitchen? In Ethan's kitchen?"

He nodded happily. "Some things are better than the old ways. You have to be able to go with what works. I whip them up into a nice pink——"

"Gumpy," she said gently, "I don't think I want to know."

He nodded, unoffended, and gazed into the fire.

A deep silence fell over them, and she felt as if there was no need for words here. The silence stretched. She became very aware of the scents in the air, the sounds of the fire crackling.

"So why?" he finally asked, breaking the long silence, "did you become a lawyer?"

Her answer astonished her. It came straight from her stomach. It did not pass through her mind. She said, "To make my parents happy."

And suddenly she could see the proud look in her father's face the day she had graduated. She realized, uneasily, her cop father still had some very old-fashioned notions about stations in life. He was inordinately pleased that she had risen above hers. He viewed her wedding to Keith in the same way. As if she was achieving all the things that had been impossible dreams for him.

"Are they?" Gumpy asked.

She was startled. "Are they what?"

"Happy?"

"They're very proud of me."

She knew she had not answered the question. Gumpy, suddenly very much Nelson Go-Up-the-Mountain, pinned her to her place with his eyes.

"So now," he said softly, "no one is happy. Not them. Not you."

"I'm happy!" she protested.

But of course she knew a perfectly happy woman never would have gotten on that airplane to a place she had never been, never would have followed a strange man out of the airport.

"When I was a little girl," she found herself telling him, "I used to dream about riding horses all the time. I rode a stick broom down the street. I had a dime-store cowboy hat. I cut out magazine pictures of horses. I wanted to come to the Calgary Stampede."

Gumpy stared thoughtfully into the fire.

"When I rode with Ethan today, I felt like that little girl again. Like those dreams never died at all, just waited inside of me. When I was on that horse, galloping, I felt like it was the only dream I ever had that was actually better than I had imagined it."

Gumpy finally spoke. "Your dreams and desires are given to you for a reason," he said. "They are not to be denied, but explored. They will tell you what you need to know about yourself. They will lead you to your true self. To your joy."

Tears spilled out her eyes. Where were all these unwieldy emotions coming from? Had they been as trapped within her as her dreams? She wiped at the tears impatiently. "That is beautiful," she told him softly. "Is that one of your Native beliefs?"

Gumpy looked sheepish. He took a sudden interest in

unwrapping his cookie.

"Oprah," he told her.

Ethan set down the phone. It looked as though Bill Justin's mother was going to be able to come and help him out for a while.

She met all the requirements. She was old. She cooked roast beef and potatoes.

Bill was going to let him know in a few days.

Ethan rubbed wearily at his eyes. He should be jumping for joy.

But the only time he had felt joy in a long, long while was riding up to the ridge with Lacey. Real joy. Something beyond contentment. Something that leaped in his blood like fire.

It had been stupid to listen to Gumpy.

He'd seen Lacey head out toward Gumpy's after she'd put the twins to bed. He hoped she would have the good sense not to be listening to him.

Could you have stopped him?

Somehow it had been in his mind all these years that he should have stopped Bryan from getting on the bull that day. Her simple question had led him to really consider the answer.

Could you have stopped him?

No. Nobody had ever been able to stop Bryan from doing what he wanted to do. He wondered why he had told her about Bryan, and he knew there was more to it than her coming across those old photos.

It had something to do with her crying yesterday. Riding old Chief and crying her heart out.

She'd shown him a little glimpse of her soul.

And maybe, by telling her about Bryan, he'd shown her a little glimpse of his.

He thought of her holding up that dress in the basement. He had seen instantly that it would fit her perfectly.

He had known what she would look like in it.

Doreen's announcement that his mother intended it as a gift for his bride had followed so closely on his mental picture of Lacey in the dress, he had nearly reeled in shock.

Tomorrow Lacey had seven days left.

His mind ordered him to go away for seven days. She could manage the kids, and Gumpy could manage the ranch.

There was something warring within him stronger than his mind.

Instinct. Pure gut feeling. And his gut told him not to be a fool.

He'd been given seven more days, a gift, and he'd better grab that gift with both hands.

Besides, without knowing it, Lacey was teaching him how to manage those kids. Today, when Doreen had looked as if she planned to pester them to eternity on getting married, he'd told her that was enough, and she had listened! Without crying!

The phone rang.

Ethan stared at it. What if it was Bill calling back already? What if his mother could come right away?

He grabbed the phone. "Yeah?"

It wasn't Bill. It was worse.

"You want what? My pro rodeo membership number? For what reason?" He listened with disbelief. "I'm riding in what? An indoor rodeo? I think you've made a mistake. Pardon? Oh. Nelson Go-Up-the-Mountain. I should have known. Can I call you back tomorrow?"

Ethan set down the phone and gave his head a slow shake.

Honestly, these days that aggravating old man made life so interesting, a guy hardly had time to catch his breath.

Chapter Seven

The house was dark and silent when Lacey came in from her visit with Gumpy. She felt alive and energized and not at all ready to go to sleep

As she hung up her jacket, she contemplated the possibility that her dreams and desires would lead her to her true self.

She stopped in the kitchen to get a pen and a piece of paper, checked on the twins and kissed each of their round cheeks. She tiptoed by Ethan's closed door, resisting the impulse to stop and listen. For what? His breathing? Really, she was becoming pathetic. She went to her room and shut the door. Firmly.

She sat cross-legged on her bed and let loose her hair, which was mostly loose anyway. Absently she ran the fingers of one hand through the tangles and looked down at the blank piece of paper in her hand.

After a few minutes, she took up the pen and across the top of the paper she wrote firmly: "Everything I Have Ever Wanted to Do."

Then, hitting a particularly nasty knot in her hair, she wrote "cut my hair."

The truth was, she had wanted to cut her hair since she was about sixteen years old. But other people adored it. Her mother. Her father. Her girlfriends. Every time she even mentioned cutting her hair, she got it from all sides. No! Don't! How can you even think such a thing?

She had mentioned it once to Keith, and he had actually paled before her eyes and said, "Lacey, your beautiful hair. Have you lost your mind?"

She decided not to get bogged down, and looked at her paper again. She wrote, list style:

ride horses
be a teacher
have babies
go to a rodeo
swim naked
dance
laugh more
make mistakes
take chances

She looked at her list and tried to decide if she still wanted to go to a rodeo. Maybe not, if Ethan's best friend had been killed at one. Still, she couldn't quite bring herself to cross it off. She decided to think about it. It was just a list, after all, not reality.

She read through the list two or three times, enjoying it very much, especially the one about swimming naked, which seemed delightfully naughty to her.

The last item on her list caught her attention every time. It challenged her. Maybe because the list wasn't reality, she added with bold flourish:

kiss Ethan

And then she laughed. She studied her list and put firm, black check marks beside "ride horses" and "laugh more." She read the list again, and the laughter left her. Where, on this list, did it say anything about becoming a lawyer? A divorce lawyer? Or anything about a big house?

Or anything about a loveless marriage?

Loveless. The word echoed inside her brain, shocking her.

She didn't love Keith. Somehow she had never even paused to ask herself that. They'd been caught up in a whirlwind of activity, surrounded by a pink cloud of other people's approval.

She liked Keith and respected him enormously.

She lived in a world that respected the pragmatic, honored it above things of the heart.

In that moment of absolute clarity, she knew, finally, why she had gotten on that plane. Her soul—her true self, as Gumpy called it—had taken charge. It knew something of her that she had not known of herself. Lacey McCade would not have been able to live without love. Perhaps she could have survived, but she never would have been alive in the way she wanted to be alive.

She looked at her list:

kiss Ethan

Oh, God. Where was all this leading her? Suddenly, instead of feeling exhilarated by all the possibilities life held, she just felt afraid. Scared witless. And exhausted.

She crumpled up her note and threw it on the floor. She undressed, crawled under the blankets and slept.

* * *

"I got an interesting call from the Sheep River Rodeo Society last night," Ethan said casually to Gumpy. Lacey put a platter of bacon on the table and shot Ethan a look. She was starting to know him well enough to know when there was a little edge to his voice.

The problem with writing down "kiss Ethan" last night in a moment of mad whimsy was that her mind somehow didn't register the part about it not being reality. Every time she looked at his lips this morning, she felt an absurd tingling way down deep in her belly. She couldn't even bring herself to join them at the table, finding all these other things that had to be done. Immediately.

Gumpy tucked into his bacon and eggs. "Oh?" he said, just as casually. "Lacey, come eat. I don't think the salt and pepper shakers have to be refilled right now."

Lacey was starting to know Gumpy well enough to know when he was up to something. She ignored him, dragging out the job, listening.

"Doreen," Ethan said, "please don't eat with your hands. It seems, Gumpy, I've been signed up for the bull-riding event at the upcoming indoor rodeo."

Lacey whirled and stared at him wide-eyed. Then she looked at Gumpy, who rocked his chair back and looked thoughtful. She noted, absently, that Doreen was eating with utensils.

Finally Gumpy said, "Oh, that. Lacey, would you come sit down?"

"That?" Ethan probed.

"It's just a little rodeo. They won't have very good bulls there."

"I haven't ridden a bull for years!"

"The gate will be bigger if you ride. More people will

come if they have a chance to see the two-time Canadian champion come out of retirement.''

Two-time Canadian champion? Lacey thought, a little dazedly. Perhaps the rumors that Alice Dempsey, the bedazzled store clerk, had heard had not been so exaggerated after all. Did it make his lips seem even more kissable?

Ethan looked narrowly at Gumpy. ''And why do you care how big the gate is?''

''A portion of it is going for charity.''

''What charity?''

''There's this program starting in the high schools. Native people, elders, are going to talk to the young people about what it is to be Native American. How prejudice hurts the whole world. About our ways. Traditions. Beliefs. Customs.''

Ethan drew in a long breath. ''What Native elders?'' he asked, the edge gone from his voice, replaced by reluctant amusement.

Gumpy cast Lacey a look. ''I guess you're not planning on eating with us today?''

''What Native elders?'' Ethan repeated.

''Me.''

''Why would that cost money?'' Ethan asked, a small smile tugging at those kissable lips. ''As far as I can see, you've always talked for free.''

''Well, of course I'll talk for free,'' Gumpy said indignantly. ''But I'll be traveling all over the province. I might need some lunch money. Bus fare.''

''You've found your calling in life,'' Ethan said.

Gumpy looked pleased. ''So, you'll ride?''

''Okay. Okay. I'm in.'' Ethan held up his hands in mock surrender, and then added so softly that Lacey almost didn't hear him, ''Grandfather.''

Gumpy nodded with satisfaction. "Before you always rode for you. A man needs to learn to give something back before he can learn how to love."

"Quite a leap from the back of a bull to love," Ethan said dryly.

She whirled away from them, knowing the sudden violent pounding of her heart would show in her face. Ethan up against two thousand terrifying pounds of mean sneaky bull? Not some nameless cowboy who looked good in his tight jeans. Ethan. Her Ethan.

Her Ethan whose best friend had been killed by a bull. Killed.

Danny looked up from his breakfast and said, "Can I go watch? Mommy says watching Unca Ethan ride bulls is like watching poultry."

Gumpy snickered.

"I think she meant poetry, honey," Lacey said, trying to keep her face calm and cool. "When is the rodeo?"

"Next weekend," Gumpy said. "That picture of you riding Honky-Tonk Demon is on the poster, Ethan. I'm surprised you ain't seen it."

Lacey would still be here. And she suddenly knew, like it or not, she was about to see her first rodeo.

Of course, she didn't have to go. What a joke. If Ethan was riding, she would not be able to stay away.

"Can we go?" Doreen and Danny chorused.

"Oh, sure," Ethan said. "Why not?"

Why not? What if you get killed, why not! "Are you sure it's appropriate entertainment for small children?" she asked nervously.

Gumpy and Ethan both looked at her as if she'd grown a second head.

"'Course it's 'propriate for kids," Gumpy said. "They can go in the mutton bustin' if they want."

"Mutton busting?" she asked.

"It's for kids too little to get bucked off steers," Ethan explained. "They get bucked off sheep, instead."

Lacey looked at them all. "They get bucked off sheep? Can't they get hurt?"

She got the growing-a-second-head look again.

"Usually just dirty," Ethan said.

"Usually?" Surely that wasn't a note of hysteria in her normally well-modulated voice?

"Lacey," Gumpy told her soothingly, "you worry too much. I told you."

She sniffed. There wasn't another salt or pepper shaker in this whole house. She took off her apron, hung it up and marched down the hall to her bedroom.

She sat on her bed. After a while, she picked up her crumpled list off the floor. Take chances, she read.

So, out here in the West, in this rugged ranch country, they taught these kids early to take chances. That sometimes life hurt. That you got up, brushed off the dust and tried again.

Suddenly she felt just a little bit homesick. She crumpled the paper again, and aimed it at her garbage can. A three-pointer if she'd ever seen one.

She thought if she never saw another cowboy, Indian, horse or twin in her life, it would be too soon.

"Lacey," two little voices called plaintively outside her door half an hour later. "What are you doing? Aren't we going to make muffins this morning?"

She pulled herself together, pasted a smile on her face and opened the door.

She had lied to herself. The truth was that she could never see enough of them. All of them.

The kitchen was empty when they made their way there.

"Did Gumpy and Ethan go to work?" she asked.

"Gumpy did. Unca Ethan had to go see a guy named Bill's mommy," Doreen told her.

"About a keeper house," Danny informed her. "What's that?"

A housekeeper. And not a moment too soon. "Nothing, sweetheart," she said. "What should we put in the muffins? Bananas and chocolate chips, or blueberries?"

Ethan had been gone all day.

A hell of an interview, Lacey thought. Gumpy had looked exhausted at supper and excused himself right after playing two games of crazy eights with the twins.

Now the twins were in bed, and Lacey sat in the darkened living room, considering that maybe she would be leaving before the rodeo.

Maybe she would never know if he lived or died.

She felt she would know. Even if she was back in California, she felt she would know the moment his spirit left the earth.

Which was a ridiculous way for a lawyer to think.

Remember that, she told herself. You are a lawyer, not a nanny.

Impatient with herself and the meanderings of a mind that suddenly did not seem to be at all disciplined, she went and fiddled with the radio. She found a station blasting rock music. She might as well not have thrown that list away, because it seemed to be emblazoned on her brain.

Dance.

Well, why not? She was a million miles from nowhere, alone in this house except for two sleeping five-year-olds. She'd put it on that stupid list. Why not just show herself how stupid the list really was?

She had never danced. At school dances she had put up the decorations and helped play the music, served hot-dogs and covertly studied those uninhibited enough to let themselves go.

Keith had been delighted when she told him she didn't dance because he didn't, either.

The music rocked. It was an old song. One she recognized. Something about jumping. She began to sway nervously. She closed her eyes and tried to feel the beat inside herself. She shuffled her feet a little. She swung her arms a little.

There was nothing so great about dancing. It was kind of boring. That whole list was probably full of disappointments, just like—

"What are you doing?"

She shrieked and turned.

Ethan was standing in the doorway, the light from the hall falling over his big shoulder. She tucked her hair nervously behind her ears and jammed her hands into her pockets.

"Nothing," she said.

"It looked like something." There was a smile in his voice. Her worst nightmare. She'd made a fool of herself.

"I thought I was by myself."

"That's when you dance? When you're by yourself?"

"I wasn't dancing, exactly."

"It kind of looked like dancing."

"Well, it wasn't. I've never danced. I mean, I've wanted to, but I never have."

He regarded her for a long time, and then he came across the floor and towered over her.

"Lacey McCade," he asked, exasperation in his voice, "have you ever done one single thing you wanted to?"

"What do you mean?" She looked up at him defiantly.

Nothing in her voice betrayed how gorgeous she thought his eyes looked, flashing silver in the deep shadow of the living room.

"Don't use that lady lawyer voice on me. Just answer the damned question."

"You saw my list," she said accusingly.

"What list?" he asked, genuinely baffled.

"Never mind."

He went over and turned up the radio. He turned back to her. He was dressed slightly differently than normal, a fancy Western shirt tucked into pressed jeans.

"You'll wake the twins," she said nervously. The shirt had wild horses on the yoke, collar and cuffs. The rest of it was plain white. A very attractive shirt. A sensible woman could study it for a good long time instead of looking at his lips.

"I doubt it. They sleep like a pair of rocks. Come on."

"Come on and what?" She looked at his lips.

"Dance."

"What?"

"We're going to dance."

"You and me?" She licked her own lips nervously.

"I don't see anyone else here. Should I go ask Gumpy if he'll dance with you?"

Yes. It would be far easier to dance with Gumpy, to risk looking the fool with Gumpy than with the handsome man who looked across the shadowed room at her, his gray eyes hooded, his lips firm and stern, and sensuous.

"I'll look stupid," she said in a small voice. She suddenly found her toes interesting.

He crossed to her in a single stride. "Stupid?" he said, amazed. He lifted her chin and she found herself looking into gray eyes that snapped with impatience. "You're more beautiful than a goddess. You couldn't look stupid if you tap-danced at the rodeo in your bikini.''

"I don't own a bikini," she said faintly.

You're more beautiful than a goddess, her mind echoed.

He growled. "But I'll bet you've always wanted to, haven't you?"

"Maybe." You're more beautiful than a goddess. They were dazzling words. Words she should have heard from her fiancé. Even once. "I can't, Ethan. I can't dance."

She pulled back from the hand resting on her chin, and it fell to his side.

"Bull."

"Well, you're an expert on that, apparently."

"That's right, I am. You can. Dance."

"Okay, I won't." She folded her arms over her chest.

He took in the stubborn stance, ran a hand through his short, silky hair. "I'll close my eyes. I won't look at you. I promise."

She bit her lip. Now it was becoming harder to say no. Much harder. Because she could watch him, but he couldn't watch her.

Plus, being more beautiful than a goddess awakened something in her. Some little part of her that thought maybe she could dance.

"All right," she whispered. "Close your eyes."

He did. He closed his eyes and began to move to the pounding rhythm of the music. He danced the way he did everything else, with an inborn certainty about himself, about his body and the way it worked. He danced with an easy, comfortable confidence. He danced as if he heard the drums of his ancestors right down in his soul.

She listened to the music and the primal beat called to

something in her. She closed her eyes and began to move. "Don't look," she warned him.

"I promised."

She began to sway, to let the music take her. It felt good. Slightly wild, and invigorating. Sensual. Very sensual.

Just as she was really getting the hang of it, Ethan crashed into the coffee table.

She stopped and laughed. He righted himself and looked at her. "Do you think I could dance with my eyes open now?"

Wide-eyed, she nodded. "All right."

He shoved the coffee table out of the way. And she danced with him. They danced until they were breathless. She laughed with the pure freedom of letting go.

In her mind she checked another item off her list. And it wasn't boring at all.

Lacey laughed again. Another song came on, the rhythm fast and hard. "I've got to stop," she finally said. "I can't breathe. I feel as if I've run a mile."

The song came to an end.

They stood there, looking at each other. She watched his chest rise and fall beneath his shirt. She felt the laughter in his eyes.

The radio announcer said he was going to play two Celine Dion songs.

Please, not "The Power of Love," Lacey thought.

The opening bars of "The Power of Love" came on.

Ethan said, "I was ready for something slower." And then he opened his arms to her.

She went into them, a winged thing accepting an invitation to celebrate the wind. She could not have refused his invitation. She could not, held now by some force entirely out of her control. His arms closed around her.

She was home.

His hold was both powerful and tender. She could feel his heart beating against her own. His scent tickled her nostrils and delighted her senses. She glanced up at him before nestling her head in the hollow of his throat. His eyes were closed.

The music wrapped around her, bound her to him, sang to her soul. Her body melted into his. She could feel his hardness, his strength right under her fingertips.

They held tight to each other, barely moving, like two people who had been shipwrecked. Like two people who had searched forever for a safe haven but not known what they searched for.

Not until now. This moment of finding.

The song ended, but he did not let her go, and the next song melted into the first one.

Barbra Streisand and Celine began to sing "Tell Him."

She had thought, once before, when she had ridden up to the ridge with him, that she was in heaven.

Now she knew she had not even been close.

For it could not get more heavenly than this, her body touching his, the music singing her thoughts all around them, the room dark and romantic.

Only last night Gumpy had told her her desires would lead her to her true self—to her joy.

She did not know if he meant the kind of desire that now caught on fire within her.

She only knew she desired this man.

More than she had ever desired anything. Food. Water. Shelter. What she longed for now was more than those things, the seed of life itself hidden somewhere in her desire.

She only knew she had waited all her life for this moment of surrender. Complete surrender.

She pressed herself tighter against him and felt his hand push her yet closer into the wall of his chest. She tilted her head, and looked up at him.

Into the deep gray of his eyes and the full sensuous line of his lip. She reached up her hand and traced his high, proud cheekbones, then touched his bottom lip.

His eyes never left hers. His lip moved on her finger. Soft. Sensuous.

Kiss Ethan.

A wave curled around her and took her. She replaced the place on his lips where her finger had rested with her lips.

She tasted him. And he tasted of things she had never known. Of wild delights. Of heaven and earth. Of everything that was meant to be between a man and his woman.

He tasted her back, his lips claiming her tenderly, like the first drops of rain before the storm. But the storm was coming, and his kisses reflected that, becoming less tender and more demanding, pelting down with a kind of hungry fury.

She answered him, as hungry as he. Starving.

Her restless hands found his shirt buttons and wrested them open. Her hands slipped inside his shirt and felt the sinewy satin of his skin under her fingertips.

Something was happening inside of her. The storm was building in intensity.

Without ever taking her lips from his, she peeled back his shirt from his arms and dropped it to the floor. Her greedy hands could not get enough of the feel of his skin, of his muscles, of his power.

"Lacey," he groaned. "If we don't stop—"

"Don't stop," she breathed. "Ethan, don't you dare stop."

He did stop, though, and scanned her face, looking to see if she really meant it.

And then his surrender was as complete as hers. He gathered her close, and then with a growl of wanting and desire he scooped her up in his arms, strode down the hall and into his bedroom, slamming the door shut with his heel.

He put her down on the bed and covered her body with his own. His mouth was all over her. Raining kisses on her hair and her ears and the hollow of her throat.

And then his hands found the buttons to her shirt and flicked them open. His hand found the gentle mound of her breast.

She shivered, delighted, terrified.

"Lacey?" He pulled his weight up on his elbows and looked down at her.

"It's okay." Her voice trembled as if she was on the verge of tears.

"Are you sure?" He reached up and touched her nose with his fingertip, a tender smile tilting his lips.

"I'm sure. I just—"

"Just what?"

"I'm a little scared."

"Of me?"

"Of course not!"

"Then—" Understanding dawned on his face. "Lacey, have you done this before?"

She blushed fire-red. "I'm thirty years old," she said.

"Don't try any of that lawyer double-talk on me. Just answer the question."

She tried to pull him back down.

He resisted, a look of astonishment dawning on his face. "Oh, Lacey."

"I want you," she whispered fiercely.

He rolled off her, and sat up on the edge of the bed. He cradled his head in his hands and took a few deep breaths. Then he turned and very gently did up the buttons on her blouse.

"Not like this," he said gruffly.

"Not like what?" she asked, desperately humiliated.

"Lacey, you've been waiting all your life for something. You don't even know me."

Didn't know him? How could he think that? How could she not know him when she had seen him tame a horse with his touch and gentle those twins with his voice? How could she not know him when she had seen him honor Gumpy over and over again? How could she not know him when she had ridden through the snow with him and felt the warmth of his hands on her ears?

Maybe what he was really saying was that he did not know her.

How could he not?

And yet she knew he was right. She had lived all her life in a world that honored the pragmatic, and she knew it was not possible to love him after such a short time together.

Never mind what her foolish heart was crying.

Her sensuality had built up in her like a dam ready to burst. And now it felt like there was a leak in the dam. And she was going to plug that with her finger?

He was giving her a chance to make her exit with pride and dignity. Surely she had enough strength left in her to take what he was offering?

He was rejecting her.

She knew she could push him over the edge with one

more small kiss. She knew it. She could feel that power within her.

But what about tomorrow?

Girl, she ordered herself, get out.

She sat up, fiddled with the last of her buttons, hiding her face from him behind the curtain of her hair. Her hands trembled.

"Of course you're right," she said brightly. "I hardly know you. You don't know me. Good grief. No wonder I never danced before!"

"Lacey, don't make it into a joke."

The smile trembled on her lips. She flounced up off the bed, pushed past him, and went out the door, refusing to look back.

In her bedroom she looked at herself in the mirror and liked what she saw. A woman. Passionate. On fire with life. Alive.

On her bed were a pair of scissors she had used to trim the twins' bangs today.

She picked them up and looked in the mirror again. She picked up the first long tress of her hair and snipped it, right beneath her ear. And then she snipped another and another.

A virgin. Ethan stared at the ceiling, his arms folded behind his head. He could hear her in her room moving around, and he wanted desperately to go to her, to explain.

But tonight, that would only lead to one place. One place he couldn't go with Lacey.

Things had happened so fast. Gone from A to Z, skipping everything in the middle. Or maybe that wasn't quite true. The middle had been the past few days.

He'd truly come to know her. He knew how she would

smile when the twins did or said something, knew how her eyes lit up when the horse started to lope, knew he could tell her things he had never told another living soul and she would understand what to do with that telling.

He should have given some thought before to whether or not he was going to sleep with her if he had the opportunity.

Be honest, he told himself. He'd thought about it, and answered that question with a resounding *yes* every single time it popped into his head.

Of course, that was before he'd known the facts. A virgin.

He didn't even know how that was possible. To look like her, and to come from a place where people played fast and hard, how could she possibly be thirty years old and a virgin? But when he had looked in her eyes, he had seen it absolutely, undoubtably. She was.

And he should be nothing but thankful. Because she was not the kind of woman a man could have once and walk away from. She was not the kind of woman a man could have a fling with and then go on as if nothing had happened.

Just his luck. He hadn't even had his one night, or the fling, and he already had the awful feeling that he was not going to be able to go on with his life as if nothing had happened.

She had happened. She had come like a breath of fresh air into a life gone stale. She had made the beat of his heart feel different. Brand-new. Young. Full of hope.

It was Gumpy's fault he'd let her close enough to do that. A man should listen to his own early-warning system.

He'd known she was trouble from the first second he'd laid eyes on her.

He'd known if he got even a little bit close to her it was going to hurt.

He hadn't known it was going to hurt her, too.

Okay. He had a chance to do the decent thing. Bill's mother could start right after the weekend.

He could tell Lacey to go now. He and Gumpy could manage a few days without her.

Someday she'd thank him that he hadn't taken advantage of her during a moment of heat she might have regretted later.

Sure. She'll probably send you a thank-you card from California.

Her life was a whole world away. That was what he had needed to remember and had forgotten the instant her lips touched his.

That she was from a different world.

That she wasn't staying and that he wasn't leaving.

That she was on the run from something she had never explained.

For a man who had done the right thing, the honorable thing, the sensible thing, he wondered why he felt so damned miserable.

Chapter Eight

"Geez," Gumpy said grouchily from where he had planted himself at the kitchen table. "I don't know what's going on this morning. I come in and the radio's goin' real loud, and then when I went to turn it off, I tripped over your shirt and nearly kilt myself."

Ethan kept his back carefully turned. He put bread in the toaster.

"No breakfast. I had to make coffee. Instant. I hate instant," Gumpy muttered.

"You'll live," Ethan said. He dared not turn around. Gumpy read him all too well, and when he had looked at himself in the mirror this morning, he had seen a changed man.

Fire and passion burning a little too close to the surface.

"I put your shirt there on the counter. It's your good one, I saw. It's not like you to leave your clothes lyin' around and—"

He stopped so abruptly Ethan chanced a careful glance over his shoulder.

Gumpy sat frozen, his coffee cup halfway to his lips, his eyes on the doorway. Ethan followed his gaze. His mouth fell open.

"Good morning," Lacey said brightly. "I must have slept in a bit. I can whip up some pancakes in about three minutes."

She said that just as nonchalantly as if she hadn't shed a few yards of hair somewhere during the night.

"I'm having toast," Ethan said. Gumpy's dark eyes fixed suddenly on his face. He turned back to the counter. The toast popped. Burned black.

"What happened to you, Lacey?" Gumpy sputtered.

Ethan pretended he didn't care, hadn't even noticed her hair. He slathered butter on the burned toast.

"I cut my hair," she said with a bright smile.

He took a bite of his toast, still standing at the counter, hoping it would keep the question down his throat where it belonged.

He had to spit out the toast.

And the question.

"What does this have to do with last night?" He had meant to sound nice and casual. His voice sounded like a grizzly growl.

"Last night?" she asked, all wide-eyed innocence.

"Last night?" Gumpy echoed.

Ethan took his toast and dumped it in the garbage. He busied himself with the instant coffee instead. The sugar was on the table. He turned to get it.

Gumpy was eyeing the counter, where the shirt lay like a dead thing. Ethan managed to get the sugar, but not before Gumpy treated him to a lethal look, like a proud papa on his way to get the shotgun.

Ethan put three teaspoons of sugar in his coffee before he remembered he didn't use sugar. He looked at her expectantly.

"Last night? It doesn't have anything to do with last night. I've always wanted to cut my hair," she told them brightly. "Ethan, could you move? You're in my way."

"What's this sudden panic to do everything you ever wanted to do?" Ethan asked. He moved only slightly. She had to touch him to reach up and get the pancake mix. She blushed, not as immune to him as she wanted him to believe.

"I guess I'm just ready for some changes," she said.

He took a sip of his coffee, which truth be told was worse than the toast, and sneaked a peek at her. She looked gorgeous. The short hair was like a cute little mop of feathers all around her face. Her bone structure was exquisite, and it showed to best advantage now.

Way in the back of his mind he remembered he'd decided what to do last night. He could feel his resolve wavering like a mirage of water on a hot day.

He forced himself to say, "I've hired a new nanny."

She didn't meet his eyes. "Great," she said. "When can she start?"

Gumpy groaned suddenly and loudly, and they both turned to him. He had grabbed his arm at the shoulder and was doubled up.

Lacey raced to Gumpy's side. She really had about the nicest neck Ethan had ever seen on a woman. Not that he'd seen that many.

Lacey crouched beside Gumpy. "What's wrong?"

"My arm hurts," he gasped.

"Your arm? Not under your arm?" She sent Ethan a swift look, and he saw the real terror in her eyes. She mouthed, "Heart attack?"

He shook his head and took advantage of her attention being elsewhere to dump his coffee down the sink.

"I fell over that fool shirt this morning," Gumpy said. "Maybe I broke it. My arm, that is."

Ethan had personally watched Gumpy somersault from horses, wrangle cattle, be trampled by bulls. And he'd never had a scratch. A broken arm from tripping over a shirt?

But Lacey was rolling up his shirtsleeve with gentle concern, while Gumpy moaned.

"Careful," Ethan muttered, "the medical missionaries will be here in a minute."

Lacey gave him a dirty look, but Gumpy smiled swiftly, then hid it when she looked back at him.

"I'll be fine," he said bravely. "I'll just lie down on the couch for today."

"That's a good idea," Lacey said sympathetically.

"But who will help Ethan feed the cattle?" Gumpy asked. Innocently.

Ethan closed his eyes.

"He'll manage," Lacey said, apparently all her compassion used right up on that old man. Couldn't she tell he was faking? What kind of lawyer was she?

"Maybe you could help him?" Gumpy said, smiling his sweetest toothless smile for her.

"Me?"

"I could watch the kids."

"But I don't know anything about feeding cattle!"

"It's not brain surgery," Gumpy told her. "You could just drive the truck."

"But I don't know how to drive that truck!"

"Ethan will show you. Won't you, Ethan?"

Why not? He could have a private moment with her. Apologize for last night. Tell her her services were no longer required. Maybe he would even drive her to the airport as soon as they were done the cattle.

His heart dropped as if it had taken an eight-story plunge on a roller coaster.

So, then again, maybe not.

After breakfast Gumpy limped to the couch. Ethan refrained, just barely, from asking him how hurting his arm had affected the way he walked.

Gumpy lay down with a theatrical moan that brought Lacey running with an ice pack. "Ethan, could you bring me a dish towel? I'll make a sling."

When Ethan came back in, Gumpy had cast his good arm over his forehead and peeked out from under it.

"So what did you do with your hair, Lacey?" he asked.

She grinned at him patiently. "I told you, I cut it."

"I can see that. I ain't senile. But what do you do with the hair?"

"The actual hair?"

"Yup. Can I have it?" Gumpy asked eagerly.

Ethan handed her the tea towel. She folded it several ways before he took it back from her and persuaded it to be a passable sling.

"What do you want her hair for?" Ethan snapped.

"Tie flies," Gumpy said, wounded.

"Tie flies?" she asked, horrified. "You mean like houseflies?"

"Sure," Gumpy kidded her along. "I catch a whole passel of them, and then I tie them up and feed them to my pet frog."

Ethan looked at her wide eyes. Did she have to do this right now? Show him what a complete big-city woman she was? Show him that, despite a law degree that hung

in an office somewhere, she had maintained her innocence?

In more ways than one, not that he wanted his mind
to go there right now.

"He means tying flies for fishing," he told her.

"Oh." She blushed and then laughed and said to
Gumpy, "Well, you keep that pet frog away from me, or
I'll be feeding you frog's legs."

"Not so rough," Gumpy complained as Ethan adjusted
the sling.

Danny and Doreen came in, looking tousled and
sleepy. Their eyes lit right up when they saw Gumpy.

"Is he really sick?" they asked eagerly.

"Really," Ethan said, showing no mercy. "And you
two can look after him all day."

Lacey actually felt light-headed. And not because she
was walking with Ethan toward the truck. Because her
head was so light after losing all that hair.

She had looked at herself in the mirror this morning,
wondering if she would feel regret. Instead, she had
looked at her reflection and felt as though she was herself.
Finally.

She did feel some regret over flinging herself at Ethan
like that. Good grief. But she'd learned something, too.
Sometimes life hurt. You got up and brushed off the dust.
She wasn't so sure about the tried again part, though.

At least he'd had the decency not to mention it. Of
course, she had rehearsed what she would say if he did
mention it.

"Lacey," he said quietly. "I'm sorry about last night."

"Oh," she said, "a healthy man and a healthy woman
under the same roof. Is it so surprising?" Her tone and
delivery were perfect. Smooth. Uncaring. Faintly amused.

He looked annoyed. "Sometimes, just when I think it's not possible, you prove to me you really are a lawyer."

"What does that mean?"

"You're putting what happened last night down to health?"

"Well?"

"I don't think it was about health."

"What then?"

He looked at her, shook his head, sighed. "Your hair looks real good like that, Lace."

He wouldn't make such a bad lawyer himself. A classic diversionary tactic.

It almost worked. He liked her hair. He'd called her Lace. It sounded almost like an endearment. But she had hoped for something else.

She snorted at herself. What? A profession of undying love? Even she knew it wasn't that. She was proud of herself for knowing. Some foolish women let lust masquerade for love. She knew. She'd handled all their divorces.

He opened the passenger truck door, and waited. He was being a perfect gentleman, just like last night. She wondered if it would wipe that impassive look off his face if she stepped on his toe. Hard.

Boldly going where she had never gone before, she pushed over to the middle seat instead of scrunching up by the window. She thought that might work nearly as well as stepping on his toe.

He got in. His leg touched hers. She studied his profile. It remained impassive, though he didn't move his leg away. She knew having failed to get a reaction from him, she should move. But she didn't.

"When's the new nanny starting?" she asked. Maybe

there was time. If she had a heart that belonged to these wide-open spaces, she needed to know that.

If she had a heart that belonged to him.

He seemed to take a sudden interest in the gauges. After a long time he said, "She can start in about a week. Can you stay until she starts?"

Obviously he was not going to be feeling an overwhelming desire to kiss her every time he passed her in the hall. Or he would have tried to get rid of her right away.

Wouldn't he?

"I guess I could."

Or maybe he was going to brush off the dust and try again. The thought made her heart race. What was one more week in the search for truth? A truth she had been searching for her entire life. A truth that maybe didn't have as much to do with discovering how he felt about her as discovering what she felt about herself. And everything else.

"What's she like?" she asked.

"Who?"

"The new nanny."

"Old."

"Is she nice?"

"Yeah. She looks like the little granny with the canary in Bugs Bunny."

"Will Danny and Doreen like her?"

"I guess."

"Will Gumpy?"

"Probably have her off to square dancing with him every Thursday night."

"Oh."

"That's not to say they won't miss you, Lacey—"

She damned her transparency. And what about him? He wasn't saying.

"—but you always made it plain you weren't staying."

They were at the bottom of the hill and he got out of the truck and they switched places. He didn't sit way over by the door, either.

"Okay," he said, "that thing under your left foot is a clutch."

"Clutch," she repeated obediently. His shoulder was touching hers. What did that have to do with learning to drive his darned truck?

"And this is a gearshift."

"All right." As long as she lived, she would remember the way he smelled. She drank it in deeply.

"It has five gears on it—see the drawing?"

She looked at the drawing on the gearshift knob. "Okay, five gears." She looked at his strong fingers on the gearshift, and remembered his fingers on the lace of her bra last night. She shivered.

Absently he turned up the heat and continued. "To use a gear, you have to push in the clutch. So, you're in neutral, you push in the clutch, let it out gently, and push down the gas at the same time. Got it?"

"Sure." And his voice. She'd remember his voice forever. Deep timbred. Confident—all right, sexy. Maybe she'd give up being a lawyer. Become a writer, instead. Every book could star him.

"Try it."

How could she try it? She had hardly heard a word he'd said, focused instead on some part of her heart that was memorizing him in preparation for goodbye.

A goodbye that was coming, even if it had been postponed.

Would they make love before she left?

Girl, don't be crazy.

Because even as things stood now it was going to take a long, long time to leave this cowboy behind, to dust herself off and try again.

If she gave in to the desire that stormed inside her, unceasingly, she might be able to dust herself off. Maybe. But try again?

It wouldn't be her body she gave to that cowboy, it would be her soul. Is that what she had really offered him last night? Not just her body, but something more? Her soul, her very spirit, that part so deep inside herself that she had hardly been aware it was there?

"Ready to try it?"

Apparently. And she wasn't talking about "driving no truck." What had made her agree to stay an extra week? A desire to torture herself?

It was too hot in here now and she was very nervous. She popped out the clutch and pushed down the gas. The truck lurched wildly forward before slamming to a halt. Ethan smashed his head against the windshield.

Holding his head, he gave her a look of awe. "I've never seen anybody drive that badly."

"Do up your seat belt," she told him with absolutely no sympathy. She shoved in the clutch and restarted the truck. She glanced at him. Blood was seeping through his fingers. She reached up and pried them away from his forehead.

It had been a mistake to touch him. She let go instantly.

He looked in the mirror and wiped impatiently at his forehead with his sleeve. Then he did up his seat belt. "You do up yours, too."

"Let me look."

"Put the damn truck in neutral first!"

She looked. He was right. It was just a scratch. Still,

she pulled a clean tissue from her jacket pocket and dabbed. "What is with you guys this morning?" she asked.

"I wondered the same thing. Years of wrestling cattle and riding rank horses and hardly a scratch. Now Gumpy's nursing a broken arm, and I'm bleeding. Do you think it could have something to do with you?"

"No!"

"Okay, let's try again. Clutch in. From neutral to first, slow out on that clutch. *Slow.*"

The truck bucked along for a few feet before it stalled this time. She cast him a look. She thought she might see impatience flashing in his eyes, pulling down the corners of his mouth.

Instead, he was trying not to laugh.

"What's so funny?"

"Lacey, you have no aptitude for this."

"I realize that. I never had any ambition to be a truck driver."

"Finally! We find something Lacey McCade never wanted to do."

She realized, reluctantly, that despite last night, it felt easy to be with Ethan. That she would willingly drive a truck all the days of her life, if it meant having him beside her. She banished the thought and slammed in the clutch. She roared along in first gear for five or ten yards before the truck made an awful noise and heaved to a halt.

"That didn't sound very good," she ventured into the silence. She glanced at him. He was looking out his window. His shoulders were shaking underneath his shirt.

"Are you laughing at me?" she asked suspiciously.

"No, ma'am." When he turned to her, his face was indeed solemn, but his eyes were dancing with a mirthful light.

"If you were bigger, I'd drive the truck, and you could throw the bales."

"If I was any bigger, I'd be the world's tallest woman." Not to mention oldest virgin.

"I didn't mean tall." He flexed an arm muscle for her. "I meant this stuff."

Her mouth went dry. She remembered the firm feel of those muscles under her fingertips last night, remembered acutely all the delightful ways he was different from her.

"I could try throwing the bales."

"Not while I breathe."

"Okay then, if you're going to be a chauvinist you better teach me quick, before the cows starve to death."

And so he taught her. He was gentle and patient and full of good humor and wisecracks. If the memory of last night haunted him the way it haunted her, he didn't show it.

"Okay," he finally said, "you graduate."

"Really?" she asked, delighted.

"Not that we're going to put you on the highway. But you can probably manage to drive slowly in first gear while I throw hay off the back, right?"

"Yes, I can manage that."

He went into the back of the truck, and she cautiously edged along, as he cut baling twine and pushed the bales off the back. She had just begun to really congratulate herself when she glanced back in the rearview mirror to see that he had disappeared.

She slammed on the brakes. And forgot the clutch. The truck stalled.

"Just when I was doing so well," she muttered.

She got out. Ethan was just standing up, dusting himself off. She ran back to him.

"What happened?"

"You need a bit more practice on your takeoff. When you pulled forward, I fell off."

"Oh. I'm so sorry."

"No big deal."

She looked at him closely. His shirtsleeve was torn. His forearm had a nasty abrasion on it. His forehead now had a smear of mud across it.

"Are you going to survive this?" she asked.

"I don't know," he said.

And suddenly she knew he was not talking about feeding cattle any more than she was.

He wondered, why had he gone and told her the new nanny couldn't start for a week? Honest to God, was he trying to see if he was made of steel?

He already knew he wasn't. He could hardly stand to be in the cab of the truck with her.

She made it smell sweet. It was everything he could do not to reach out and ruffle her new hairdo to see if it felt the way it looked. She had a way of catching her bottom lip between her teeth as she concentrated on driving that made him remember, acutely, what kissing her had been like.

He could hardly think straight to tell her what to do. It had been unfair to tell her she had no aptitude when his own mind was so addled he was probably teaching her all wrong. By the time he'd gotten out of the cab and started tossing bales, he felt he should be nominated for an Academy Award for the performance he was giving.

She didn't have a clue that he was thinking of kissing her. Not a clue.

He hadn't toppled off the back of that truck because she had pulled away too swiftly, either. He'd been craning his fool neck to get a better look at her in the truck's side mirror.

He'd bought himself another week. Just to look at her. To drink in her smell. To memorize her laughter. To save it all inside himself to take out and look at on those long winter nights after she was gone.

Gone. The word sneaked up on him, and hit him like a physical blow.

Lacey gone.

Maybe if he asked nicely, she would stay. Beyond a week.

Then he thought of last night.

There was only one way he could ask that woman to stay, and that was if he had forever on his mind.

And he was startled to find that he did.

"Ethan? What's wrong?"

"Hit my head harder than I thought," he muttered.

"Do you want me to look at it?"

"No!"

She had been moving toward him, and she stopped. He'd hurt her damn feelings.

"Let's get these cattle fed."

"All right." She turned and got back in the truck, peeking back at him through that mirror, her eyes huge.

Was she crying?

Well, that was the damn thing. He didn't know anything about how to make a woman happy. He'd probably be saying things all the time that would make her cry. She'd probably bust right into tears if he asked her that stupid question that was now going around and around in his mind.

Lacey McCade, would you marry me?

He groaned, and not from the effort of shoving the big

bale off with both his legs, either. Now he'd gone and done it.

A whole week more of thinking of kissing her.

A neon sign in his brain flashing on and off saying kiss Lacey, kiss Lacey, kiss Lacey. And another one saying, marry her, marry her, marry her.

She jerked the truck again, and he tumbled off the back.

The thing was, he thought, staring up at the sky, you had to keep your guard up around a woman like that. Let it down, and you were flat on your back staring at the sky before you even knew what had hit you.

He contemplated that hair Gumpy had his heart set on. The old guy was probably working some of his special voodoo on it right now.

A big old cow came and stared at Ethan curiously. She put her big wet nose down and gave him a sniff.

"It's just me," he said. "You've seen me every damn day for your whole life. Okay, from a slightly different angle."

The cow's eyes widened until they rolled white, and then she snorted fearfully.

All over his face.

He wiped cow snort off his face, got to his feet and sprinted after the truck.

Maybe, he'd give himself a day or two to see if his mind settled.

He reminded himself, as he caught the truck and swung up onto the flatbed, that she was a lawyer. A lawyer. She probably made more money in a month than he made in a year.

He didn't even know what she really dressed like, but

he was willing to bet her closet back home didn't hold much in the way of blue jeans and flannel shirts.

Marry her.

His mind did not plan to be rational about this. Not after last night. Completely drugged by a few breathless kisses.

Take a chance.

Once upon a time, his whole life had been about taking chances. The thrill of the bull and the thunder of applause had soothed some devil within him. Until Bryan died. And then he had come back here, to the foothills, his birthplace, and found in hard work in big spaces, contentment. Within himself. Acceptance, even quiet enjoyment of who he was, and of his heritage.

The wild boy he'd been never could have made a relationship work with anyone.

But now...if ever he'd been ready to share his life with someone, it was now.

He was going to have to take an even bigger chance than he'd taken lowering himself into the chute onto the back of a two-thousand-pound devil.

He'd have to ask her. Lacey, will you marry me?

The truth was, he wasn't sure if he could just come out and ask her.

He'd look for a sign. That was what he'd do. Gumpy would approve of that.

If he won that bull-riding event on Saturday, he'd ask her. Okay, she might laugh in his face. Or cry. She might say yes, too. Besides, he hadn't ridden a bull for a long, long time. What were his chances of winning?

His chances were terrible, and that was a fact. But suddenly he felt as if he had something to hope for, and he realized he hadn't felt that way in a long, long time.

When he put his shoulder to the last bale, he noticed he was whistling that song from the other night. What was it called? Oh, yeah. ''The Power of Love.''

And suddenly he felt that power stir, deep within him, in his very soul, and he knew that nothing he had ever experienced before even compared to it.

She stopped the truck and got out. She shook her new hair, and the sun caught in it, and she turned shining eyes to him. He wanted to go and take her in his arms and whirl her around and tell her this stunning truth that was inside him.

He had fallen in love. He was thirty years old, and he had just fallen in love for the first time. He might as well have been fourteen. Because he was afraid to look at her, afraid she would see it in his eyes. He shoved his hands deep in his jeans pockets and took an interest in the toe of his boot.

Ask her to marry him? He suddenly couldn't even think of one thing to say to her. Well, one thing.

''I bet Gumpy burned lunch.''

''Maybe,'' she said, also seeming to find her toe suddenly interesting, ''we could squeeze in a ride sometime today.''

He wanted nothing more than to go for a ride with her. Nothing.

But he was now a man with a long-term goal.

''I can't. I'm going to go practice riding some bulls this afternoon. A guy down the road raises Brahmas. He likes people to get on them for a little test drive every now and then.''

''Really? I had no idea bull riding was something that could be practiced.''

''Well, now you know.''

He glanced again at her eyes. She was looking at him skeptically. She didn't know. Not yet. Not everything. But she would.

Soon.

Chapter Nine

Gumpy had burned lunch. Not that he seemed to notice. He was gobbling up his toasted salmon sandwich with relish. The sling hung around his neck, but he wasn't using it. His arm didn't seem to be hurting at all anymore.

"Where did Ethan go in such a fired-up hurry?" he asked. "Couldn't even eat?"

"He said one of the neighbors had some bulls he could practice riding."

"Practice? Ethan?"

"That's what he said."

"Humph. You'd think he had something at stake. He don't really. He's donating all his prize money to me. Not that he knows it yet."

"Maybe he'll want to keep his prize money himself," Lacey suggested, amused. "If he wins."

"Oh, he'll win something. He won't care about the money, though. What's a man like Ethan need money for? He's already got everything he wants."

Lacey stared at Gumpy. It was true. She came from a

world where money was some sort of god. Every hour
billed. The bottom line worshiped. Money was the mea-
sure of the man.

But not of Ethan. He made his own rules and played
by them, and not one of them seemed to have a single
thing to do with money.

"*Almost* everything he wants," Gumpy amended
thoughtfully. "There might be one thing left. But money
can't buy that."

"And what is that?" Lacey asked, pretending she
didn't really care, was only making conversation.

"You know," Gumpy said sagely.

"Actually, I don't."

"Well, you'll just have to figure it out...."

On the Friday night before the rodeo, Lacey actually
saw Ethan. For two days there had been signs that he was
around—crumbs left on the counter in the morning, a
coffeepot half filled, leftovers gone from the fridge, a
damp towel hung neatly in the bathroom—but he had
become as elusive as a bear in winter.

Now she awoke from where she had fallen asleep on
the couch to see him, his face bathed in shadows, looking
down at her. Was that tenderness in his eyes? Had she
felt the touch of a strong hand on her cheek or only
dreamed it?

"Hi," she said groggily. "What time is it?"

"Late."

"You should have been home early. You have to ride
tomorrow."

He smiled. "Now what do you know about that?"

"You told me. You said a person has to be 100 percent
to ride a bull."

He reached out and pressed a finger to the bridge of

her nose, then let his hand drop away. "You worry too much."

"So Gumpy keeps telling me." She stretched and yawned.

"What were you doing?"

"Watching *Dances with Wolves*. I fell asleep before the end, thank God. I can't stand it when they catch him and shoot his horse and the wolf."

"Are you memorizing it?"

"Just like you and Gumpy." Especially the parts between Stands with a Fist and Dances with Wolves. Those parts absolutely made her ache.

For Ethan.

Dances with Bulls.

Dances with Bulls was wearing butter-yellow chaps strapped over his jeans tonight. He was covered in dust and muck and looked about as sexy as a man could look—who had all his clothes on.

She never used to think thoughts about men without their clothes on. Never.

His hair was flattened to his head, and the band of his hat had pressed a line into his forehead. Why did that make him look so recklessly attractive?

And happy. He looked happy.

"Things going well?" she asked him casually. She struggled to sit up. Maybe he would sit down on the couch beside her.

"Couldn't be better."

He was actually beaming. As if riding stupid, beastly bulls did more for his soul than dancing and kisses.

Well, maybe it did.

"I'm scared," she whispered.

"For me?" He looked astonished, and faintly pleased.

"I don't want you to get hurt, Ethan." She wanted to

beg him not to ride, but somehow she knew that loving Ethan was not about taming him. But about accepting him the way he was.

Loving Ethan.

Something darkened in his eyes. She almost wondered if that vulnerable thought had somehow telegraphed itself to him. He reached out his hand again, cupped her jaw and the side of her face in it. His thumb tickled her ear.

For a moment, she saw something in his face that made her heart stop.

Was it possible Ethan cared for her? Deeply?

The look vanished and his hand dropped away.

"I've got to hit the shower. I guess I don't smell so good."

She thought he smelled wonderful. Leather and animals and sweat all mingled together in the air around him. He smelled of strength and resiliency and ruggedness. It occurred to her the aftershave companies had it all wrong.

"Good night, Lace."

If he'd asked her to wait up for him she would have. But he didn't.

He was whistling as he headed down the hall to the shower.

"The Power of Love." Did that mean something?

He turned suddenly and caught her looking at the way those chaps framed his backside. She blushed.

And that audacious cowboy winked!

Seeing Ethan in his chaps had kept Lacey awake half the night, so it seemed too early when the twins zoomed into her bedroom wearing their pajamas and brand-new cowboy hats.

"Look what was on the end of our beds this morning!" Danny cried. "Do you think the tooth fairy left them?"

"Did you lose a tooth?" Lacey teased.

"The rodeo fairy then," Doreen decided. "Or maybe Unca Ethan. I'm going to wear my overalls that you gave me, Lacey."

Danny, never to be outdone, announced he would be wearing his overalls, as well.

They looked cute enough to put on a poster when they were all dressed up in their overalls, black plaid shirts and black cowboy hats.

Gumpy came in, looking very handsome in a dress Western shirt, pressed jeans, a white cowboy hat and dress boots. Around his neck was the most beautiful beaded string tie.

Lacey felt quite frumpy next to them all in her plain jeans and flannel shirt. She didn't even own a cowboy hat.

Or thought she didn't.

At her place at the table was a beautiful pure-white felt hat.

"The rodeo fairy strikes again," she murmured.

At the urging of the twins, she put it on. It felt a little silly, and a little fun, and when she looked at herself in the mirror, she was surprised how good she looked in it.

As if she'd been born to wear a hat like this.

As if she was finally herself, she thought not for the first time.

"Ethan gone already?" Gumpy asked.

"I guess so. Why would he go so early?"

Gumpy shrugged. "Cowboys are a superstitious lot. He probably didn't want anything to wreck his concentration."

"Like what?" she asked, putting her hands on her hips.

Gumpy smiled. "Like the way you look in that hat."

She couldn't help but smile, though her thoughts went immediately to Ethan and his bull ride yet to come.

Lacey thought time would drag, but almost before she knew it, she was at a huge arena, breathing in the scents, and seeing more real live cowboys than she had ever seen before. From the first moment she was entranced.

She found seats for herself and the twins. Gumpy, a huge mysterious bag over his shoulder, had wandered off almost as soon as they got in the doors of the arena.

There was something about all these cowboys.

It was the way they moved. With a certain sureness, a comfort with their own bodies, men who had tested the limits of what the human body was meant to do and had triumphed. There was a mystique about cowboys that beckoned to her spirit.

And had ever since she had been a little girl.

Now she had a name for it: cowboy heart.

The rodeo began with cowgirls on horseback, beautifully dressed in sequined shirts and colorful chaps and cowboy hats, racing out into the arena at full gallop, flags waving behind their horses.

Lacey longed to be one of them.

They halted their horses in a long row, and then a Native man came out, bareback on a paint horse. The man was in full regalia. His buckskin shirt and leggings were beautifully beaded in a diamond pattern, the brilliant colors of the sun setting—oranges and reds and yellows and a touch of purple. The beadwork pattern was repeated in the brow band of a magnificent eagle feather headdress. He wore leather gloves beaded up the high cuffs to his forearms, and soft, high moccasins.

"Oh, look, it's Gumpy!" Doreen cried.

Lacey stared, astonished. It was Gumpy.

"Hi, Gumpy!" Danny yelled into the awed silence that Gumpy's appearance had caused in the arena.

"Ladies and gentlemen," a voice boomed over the loudspeaker, "Mr. Nelson Go-Up-the-Mountain will open our rodeo today."

Gumpy lifted his arms, palms up, and raised his chin and closed his eyes. The audience rose to their feet, hands were clasped and heads bowed.

"Creator of all of us," Gumpy said, his voice loud and firm, and not in the least needing a microphone, "we ask Your protection for the competitors in today's events. We ask that in the strength and the courage of man and beast we are able to see Your glory. We ask that the barriers between races come down, that we might all know the joy of our brotherhood, of our humanity. We thank You for Your spirit in this arena and in each of our hearts."

He dropped his hands back to the leather thong reins and turned the horse in a slow circle, making eye contact with each and every person in the stands, it seemed to Lacey. And then with his back straight with dignity, he rode out of the arena.

Silence followed him and then thunderous applause.

Lacey felt a deep sense of gratitude that she had been allowed to know this very special man.

The first event was women's barrel racing, and it was absolutely gripping. Many of those same women who had carried banners now competed against a clock, sending galloping, snorting, hyped-up horses careening in a cloverleaf pattern around three barrels.

If she was staying, Lacey knew she wanted to learn how to do that.

But, of course, she was not staying.

She wondered if, from behind the chutes somewhere, Ethan was watching. Admiring those young women and their bravery, feeling, as she felt, how well suited to him they would be.

Gumpy, dressed like himself again, came and sat with Lacey and the children, bringing a box full of hot dogs with him.

"Gumpy, that was a beautiful opening for the day," Lacey told him, laying her hand on his sleeve. The aroma of the leather he had just worn still clung to him.

"Thank you," he said, passing out the hot dogs. "I practiced what I was going to say for darn near a month, and then when I opened my mouth something different came out."

Lacey laughed.

After the kids had finished their hot dogs, Gumpy took them to sign up for mutton busting, which was the next event. Lacey wanted to go, but he told her it might be better if she stayed where she was.

"Don't want to lose such good seats," he said.

Of course she knew he didn't want her running out in the dust if one of the kids was hurt, screaming and making a fool of herself.

During a break in the rodeo action, she looked around with interest.

Her cowboy hat was not the least out of place. She had never seen so many authentic-looking cowboys and cowgirls gathered under one roof.

For a moment Lacey caught sight of a very blond head moving through the crowd on a walkway on the other side of the arena.

For a moment her heart stopped.

Keith.

But, of course, it wouldn't be Keith. He had no idea where she was.

She shook her head a bit shakily. Even if Keith did

know where she was, he would probably be angry enough that he wouldn't be in the same place.

The bright blond head that had reminded her of him disappeared in the crowd and the mutton busting started.

Doreen was first.

She came out, clutching the back of a sheep, two cowboys spotting her on either side. The sheep bounced this way and that, and then simply stopped.

The crowd burst into laughter, and Doreen pounded at the sheep with her heels to no avail. A buzzer sounded, and Doreen slipped off the back of the placid sheep and gave a dramatic bow. She was beaming from ear to ear. The crowd roared their approval, and Lacey knew Doreen was hooked now.

Were there female bull riders? Doreen was probably destined to be one. That or being a medical missionary in some faraway land.

Lacey felt a stab of unwanted sadness. She could almost see her path and Doreen's parting, moving away from each other. She was probably never going to know if Doreen would make a career of riding bulls or nursing—or selling real estate, for that matter.

Her own future suddenly seemed as murky as swamp water, as uncertain as the unpredictable Alberta weather.

Thankfully, Danny came out next, pulling Lacey swiftly back into the moment. His sheep was slightly more energetic than Doreen's had been. It hopped sideways, and then threw up both its back legs. Danny held on with both hands, his brow furrowed with furious concentration that made him look like a miniature of Ethan. At the last moment Danny took one hand off the strap he had been clinging to, and waved it in the air, cowboy-style.

The applause was thunderous. Lacey put her fingers

between her teeth and whistled, something her mother had stopped her from doing when she was around fourteen.

Danny flipped off the sheep, and despite the spotters, landed face first in the dirt.

He got up quickly, more worried about his hat than his bruises. He brushed himself off and grinned. In that grin Lacey saw his future much more clearly than she could see her own.

His future and his cowboy heart.

After the competition finished, Gumpy brought Doreen and Danny back, chatting excitedly about their victories. Each had a small medal on a ribbon hanging from their necks. Spectators sitting around them made a huge fuss over them and their medals.

It seemed to Lacey each event was progressively more exciting than the last one. Saddle bronc riding was followed by bareback bronc riding.

After the bareback bronc riding, there was a break while they began loading bulls into the chutes.

Lacey was beginning to feel a little sick with bad nerves.

When the commentator announced the bull riding, she thought she was going to faint. She hoped Ethan would ride first so she could get this over with, but of course, he didn't.

On TV the bulls had never looked quite so large. Here in the arena, in such close proximity to them, she could see their beady, angry little red eyes.

The clowns' job was explained to them, and she was stunned by the danger of this sport. How could it even be called a sport? They were like gladiators down there, putting their lives on the line for entertainment.

The chute opened and the first bull exploded out. His

rider was heaved off after the second twist and the bull turned on him with menace gleaming in his eyes. The cowboy raced for the fence, the clowns right behind him. All three went up the fence a split second before the bull's horns swiped the air where they had just been.

Two men on horses emerged and calmly pushed the bad-tempered brute toward an open gate. When the bull saw it, he kicked up his heels with glee and thundered out.

Lacey's breath felt as though it was thundering in her chest.

The next rider was announced. Again not Ethan. Again relief that it wasn't him mixed with a desire to get this over with.

The second cowboy made the eight-second mark, but Gumpy told her the ride was not impressive.

She was very impressed. Maybe not with the ride, but the dismount was spectacular. The cowboy leaped off the bull's back, staggered, and before he could right himself the bull was racing toward him, murder burning in its piggy eyes.

A clown raced right in front of the bull, diverting him. Lacey squealed as the bull gained on the clown. The clown jumped in a barrel that was in the center of the arena, and the bull rammed it with all his might, sending it rolling away.

Lacey gasped and covered her eyes. She peeked out between her fingers. The bull had found the exit, and the clown came out of the barrel and walked a few drunken steps for the delighted crowd before he took a deep bow and was applauded for his bravery.

Lacey thanked God Ethan wasn't the one wearing the clown suit. Doreen took her hand, patted it, and told her not to worry so much. Danny was taking obvious pleasure in his close proximity to such unrelenting action.

The next cowboy made his eight seconds, and then got his hand caught in the rigging when he tried to dismount.

"That's how Ethan got that scar on his hand," Gumpy told her.

The cowboy's hand finally came free after he had been bounced around the arena several times by a furious bull. When his hand came free, he rubbed his shoulder and waved to the crowd.

"Probably dislocated his shoulder," Gumpy said matter-of-factly.

And then, when she glanced down toward the chutes, she saw Ethan. Looking calm and focused, lowering himself onto the back of a bull.

Her heart stopped within her chest. Her lungs no longer filled with air. Her eyelids did not blink. She stared at him, and knew.

Knew that it was not just her body she had offered him that night.

This was her man.

The one she would love for all time.

In that frozen second before the gate opened, she knew it. She wanted to laugh at the naive young woman she had been when she had asked herself what could possibly happen in two short weeks.

Now she knew eight seconds could change a whole life. It could certainly change hers. If Ethan came off that bull. Or if he went underneath it. Or if it took a run at him and gored him with its powerful horns.

She watched him. His face was calm. He adjusted the rigging over his hand, pulled, adjusted again. He said something to someone, clamped his cowboy hat down tighter on his head.

And then she saw him give a grim nod, and the chute door opened in what seemed like slow motion.

A whole life could change.

Not in two weeks.

Not even in eight seconds.

In one second.

In the one second it took to take one turn instead of another on the road of life. In the one second it took to look into the eyes of another and to feel your heart whisper it had found its way home.

"You're on deck, Black."

Ethan nodded.

A man was suddenly in front of him. A blond man. Tall, tanned. Handsome in a Hollywood kind of way.

Hollywood. Ethan had a sudden feeling of foreboding.

"Are you Ethan Black?" the man asked.

Ethan nodded, curtly, listening for the accent. California. He'd know it anywhere now.

"I'm looking for Lacey McCade."

Ethan said nothing, pulling on a leather glove with his teeth.

"I traced her down to a store here in Sheep River where she used her credit card. A man there said she might be working for you. As a nanny."

This was said with barely hidden scorn.

"Maybe," Ethan said. He looked the man dead in the eye. What was in his own gaze must not have been nice, because the man backed away from him. When he spoke again, the scorn was gone from his voice.

"My name's Keith Wilcox." He extended his hand.

Ethan took it. But he really didn't squeeze until the other man said, "I'm her fiancé." Then he put enough iron in his grip to make the other man wince and hastily grab back his hand.

He looked at Ethan with wariness. "I need to find Lacey."

Ethan thought that was just too bad. If Lacey had wanted to be found, she would have been.

But then Wilcox said, "Her father's had a heart attack."

He wanted not to believe the man in front of him. He had plans. He listened as his number was called.

He remembered Lacey going pale when she had thought Gumpy was having a heart attack. Why would she have even jumped to that conclusion unless it was a fear she had come face-to-face with in the past?

"Look, I got a bull to ride. I'll help you find her when I'm done."

"Thanks, I'd appreciate that."

Ethan said nothing.

"Is it as scary as it looks?" Wilcox asked him casually.

"What?"

"Riding the bull?"

"It don't hold a candle to most of life," Ethan said wearily. He walked toward the chute and could feel his energy draining into the ground. He knew before he climbed on the fence his concentration was shot. About 85 percent. Not good enough.

Not that it mattered now, anyway. He had nothing to come in first for.

Her fiancé.

The man's shoes had looked as though they were worth as much as a good saddle. The shirt looked like silk. Lawyers must like silk. Ethan bet her fiancé was a slick lawyer, just like her. Looked as if he made a couple of hundred grand a year. He could probably keep Lace in real style. Mansions and swimming pools and Mercedes.

He lowered himself onto the bull, wrapped his hand carefully in the rigging, tested.

And suddenly there was nothing else in the whole world except him and this bull and the next eight seconds and he was glad.

He nodded and the gate swung open.

''Pure poultry,'' Gumpy said as Ethan exploded out of the chute on the back of a pure black Brahma bull that the announcer told them was named Suicide.

And it was poetry.

As Lacey watched, she dropped her hands away from her eyes. The fear left her. She was awed at the control Ethan had, at the way his body seemed to anticipate every twist and turn of the big bull, and at the way it seemed to absorb each shock and jolt. There never seemed to be a moment when he was in danger. When the eight-second buzzer rang, she almost wished Ethan's ride could last longer.

He threw one long leg over the bull's back, and leaped down lightly. His hat had come off and he sauntered over and picked it up, keeping one eye on the bull, wary but not afraid.

He put his hat back on, dusted off his pants, and then looked at the crowd, his eyes sweeping the stands.

Until he found her.

She smiled and waved. She put her fingers between her teeth and whistled.

And even from here she could tell there was something wrong with the smile he returned. There was something sad in it. Still, he saluted her, and then he turned and with long-legged confidence strode out of the arena.

"It'll put him in the money," Gumpy decided. "I doubt it will win, though."

How could Gumpy say Ethan wouldn't win? He already had won. He was alive. He wasn't hurt. That was all she needed. She got up.

"Gumpy, you watch Doreen and Danny. I've got to go to him. I have to."

Gumpy grinned. "About damn time, too."

She felt as if she was swimming upstream, trying to get through the crowds to the chutes. She looked for him, and then suddenly saw him, coming toward her, a head higher than everyone else, walking with certainty and grace.

It wasn't until she broke by the last person that she saw who was with him. Keith. She didn't want to see Keith like this. His timing was all wrong. She didn't want to feel guilty in this wondrous moment when love had introduced itself to her. Love, not at all in the same category as the genuine liking and respect she had for Keith.

Ethan's long stride faltered, but only briefly.

Keith saw her, and his whole face brightened, before he frowned. She stared at the remote planes of Ethan's face even as she listened to Keith's voice.

"Lacey! What on earth have you done to your hair?" Keith asked. "You've just got your hair tucked up under that hat, don't you?"

She turned, reluctantly, from Ethan. "I cut it. Keith, what on earth are you doing here?" She felt as if Keith had stolen a moment that should have been hers. Hers and Ethan's. A moment that, from the icy look in Ethan's eyes, they were never going to have now. Never. She shivered.

"You used your credit card," Keith said, pleased. "That's all Tommy needed."

Tommy was one of many private investigators used by their law firm.

"Lace." Suddenly Ethan was right in front of her. He touched her chin with a hand still clad in a leather glove. "Your dad's sick. You have to go home."

She stared at him, not understanding, and then she sent startled eyes to Keith who had decided maybe now was not the best time to be pleased with his detective skills.

"His heart?" she asked slowly, painfully.

Keith nodded. "There's a plane in an hour. We could make it if we rush."

"I have to say goodbye to the twins. To Gumpy. I have to—" She was staring at Ethan, but his face was swimming in front of her eyes.

She needed him to hold her. Didn't he know that?

"I'll say goodbye to them. I'll explain." His voice had the same pure-blue ice in it that she had seen in his eyes. He had already said goodbye. To her.

She felt the tears trickling down her cheeks, and she did not know if it was the shock of learning about her father's illness, or the shock of saying goodbye to him so swiftly, with no warning.

Maybe it would be just as well if Ethan said her goodbyes for her. She would just upset the twins if she cried.

"I'll call you," she said, "when I get there." Her shoulders were heaving. Keith put an arm around her, but she could feel his discomfort at this public display, saw him casting glances around even though he didn't know a single soul there.

She broke out from under his grip and flew to Ethan. She wrapped her arms around him. He put his arms around her, one quick strong squeeze and then put her away from him.

Even through the tears, even though his face showed

nothing, she knew he was going away from her…and that she had to bring him back.

"Ethan," she said fiercely, "I did do something I wanted to do. Before I met you. I did."

A reluctant smile tugged at the corner of his mouth. "And what was that?"

"Two weeks ago," she croaked through the tears, "I got on that plane."

As she walked away, she could hear them announcing the results of the bull ride.

Ethan had placed second.

The announcer said that he had donated all his winnings to the charity and challenged all other riders to do the same.

She laughed through her tears.

"Lacey," Keith pleaded, "please get hold of yourself. And could you please take off that ridiculous hat?"

Chapter Ten

Lacey came out of her father's room and walked down the quiet corridor. Absurdly she wondered how hospitals always got their floors so shiny. The elevator swished down and brought her to the main foyer.

There were several deep leather couches facing each other, and she sat down, collecting her thoughts.

Keith had left an hour ago, saying he had some things to catch up on at the office. Somehow he had managed to convey that was her fault.

She had promised her mother she would spend the night with her. Lacey's eyes went to the clock. What time was it in Alberta?

She noticed a pay phone and decided to call now before it was too late.

As she dialed the number, she looked out the windows. Palm trees and parking lots. A part within her longed for spaces with no intrusions in them, and her eyes drifted to the sky.

A huge plane, a 747, was angling upward, and her breath caught in her throat.

A long time ago, a lifetime ago, two whole weeks ago, she had stood in the Calgary airport, watching the big planes taking off, thinking it seemed impossible that they could fly.

It had really been about her. All her life lumbering along the runway, never quite getting up to speed, never quite taking off.

And then suddenly she had been airborne. And discovered not just that she could fly, but that she was meant to fly.

She had hoped Ethan would answer the phone, but it was Gumpy.

"Hi, Gumpy, it's Lacey."

A few short hours and they were already a world apart. He sounded so close.

"How's your dad?" Gumpy asked.

"I just saw him. He's pretty good. It was not a major heart attack."

Her father had looked so pleased to see her—and a look had been exchanged between him and Keith.

Of course he hadn't masterminded a heart attack to get her home.

But he hadn't hesitated to use it.

"It's not your fault he had a heart attack. Don't feel guilty," Gumpy said gently.

She laughed a little. Guilt. Suddenly she understood that was what had kept her anchored to the ground for so long. Feeling so responsible for everything and everybody. Except herself.

"I probably shouldn't have taken off like that," she said. "He worried."

"Is your father overweight?" Gumpy asked.

"Well, yes, but—"

"Does he smoke?"

"Well, he did but—"

"Has he ever had a heart attack before?"

"Well, yes, but—"

"It wasn't your fault. Say it."

"It wasn't my fault," she said in a small voice.

"Nope. Say it like you mean it."

She laughed. "You're wonderful. Did I tell you that?"

"Say it like you mean it."

"You're wonderful."

"Not that! I knew you meant that."

"All right. It wasn't my fault." And suddenly she realized she hadn't just said it. She had felt it. It wasn't just words, it was the truth. "And it's not my fault Keith is behind at work, either."

"Damn right."

"You don't even know Keith."

"I can guess. Are you going to marry him? Ethan said that guy who came to get you introduced himself as your intended."

That explained the ice in Ethan's eyes when he had led Keith to her at the rodeo.

She sighed. In Alberta she had felt so strong. So sure of what she needed to do. But here everything seemed different. Including her. Could any of the things she felt—those incredible feelings of freedom and discovery—be real if they disappeared as soon as the climate changed?

On the airplane ride home, Keith had talked about setting a new date. He'd said they could forget the big wedding if it was too stressful for her. They could just fly to Hawaii for a weekend and do it.

"I'm not marrying you, Keith," she had told him.

Come to think of it, there had been a touch of her new-found iron in that statement.

Keith seemed to miss the iron in that answer, though. He was nothing if not confident. He seemed to think it was something she would get over given time. And pressure.

"No. I straightened it out with him. I'm not going to marry him."

"Can I tell Ethan? That's what you were running away from? Marrying a man you didn't really love?"

"Ethan won't understand."

"Why not?"

"He's never run away from a single thing in his entire life."

"You might be surprised," Gumpy muttered. "Hey, quit that!"

"Pardon?"

"Danny bit my ankle to get me to hurry up and give him the phone. Okay, okay—"

"Hi, Lacey!" She heard the sounds of a tussle, and then Doreen was on the phone. And then Danny. And then Doreen.

"You two have to stop fighting," she called over their unholy racket. "Is your uncle there?"

"No. He went to pick up the new keeper house."

"You two be nice to her."

"We will." Giggles sounded that did not bode well for the new nanny.

When she finally hung up, she noticed she was crying. She wiped away the tears and walked out the doors.

He had replaced her that quickly.

She told herself it was okay. The warm air hit her in the face. This was her reality. Already it was claiming her, pulling her back.

But she had a new message in her heart. And she knew, suddenly, she was stronger than she had ever given herself credit for. She turned around and walked back in the doors, went up the elevator and down the shiny corridor.

"I thought you'd gone home, honey," her father said.

She leaned over and kissed him, pushed the iron-gray hair back from his forehead.

"I forgot to tell you something."

"You're going to marry Keith?" he said hopefully.

"No. I came to tell you it's my life. I can't live it just to please you."

"Well, who ever asked you to?" he asked indignantly.

"You did."

"Me?"

"You've wanted me to be a lawyer since I started school."

"Well, it's a good job. And you were so smart. I didn't want you to end up in a dead-end low-level job like mine."

"Didn't your job make you happy?" she asked.

"Not really. I never really liked it. But my generation believed you got a job and you did it whether you liked it or not. You supported your family."

She looked at him sadly. His whole life spent doing what he thought he should, instead of what he really wanted.

"Dad, you're not going to like this. I don't like being a lawyer any more than you liked being a cop."

"Don't say that!"

"I think you always wanted to be a lawyer."

He smiled. "I did. That's a fact."

"I wanted to be a teacher."

"Lacey! A teacher? With your mind? Wiping noses all day?"

"I think there's a little more to the job than wiping noses."

"Humph."

"I like kids. Adore them."

"Well, you and Keith can have—"

She shook her head. "There is no me and Keith. I'm not going to marry him. I don't love him."

"What do you know about love?"

"A lot more than I knew two weeks ago. I'm a grown woman, Dad. Thirty years old. I'm not your little girl anymore."

"You'll always be my little girl. Does this mean you're going to quit law?"

"It means I have a great deal of thinking to do. About what I want from life."

"Lacey, all I ever wanted was for you to be happy."

"I know. You thought you knew what would make me happy."

"Aw, Lacey. Stick with Keith. He could give you everything your heart ever desired."

"No, he couldn't. I'm only just beginning to know what my heart desires, and it's not anything Keith could give me."

"So what does your heart desire?" her father asked, a little crabbily.

He wouldn't understand at all if she told him her heart desired a cowboy who lived half a world away.

So she just smiled. "I'll come see you again tomorrow after work."

"If you still have a job," her father said a little huffily.

He probably would have been very perturbed to know part of her wished she had been fired.

Her boss did make threatening noises at the office the next day, until she gave him thirty days' notice, and then he started begging her to stay. She shook her head and walked out of his office.

All those things she had learned in Alberta, all that strength she had discovered was still inside her, after all.

It seemed to her that if she was ever going to be the kind of person that Ethan could love, she had to honor what she knew herself to be.

She went into her office and shut the door. She ignored the profusion of pink slips that ordered her to return calls and picked up the morning paper. She scanned the For Sale ads.

Keith came in late in the morning. He entered without knocking and stood in the doorway studying her. "That haircut kind of grows on a person."

"It's great. I dried it in two minutes this morning."

"You want to go for lunch?"

"No, thanks, I've got something to do. I'm going to look at a horse."

"A horse?" he echoed.

"That's right. A horse."

"Does this have something to do with him? That man? The bull rider?"

"No. Just me. I've always wanted a horse."

"Really? Why didn't I know that?"

"It seems to me you and I never got to what was really important about each other."

"Did something happen between...well, you know."

"What makes you ask?"

"You just seem so different."

"Really?" she asked, pleased.

"Bolder, brighter, like there's a fire burning in you."

"Keith, I've never known you to be poetic."

"When I went to university, I wrote all kinds of poetry," he said. "Hard to believe now, isn't it?"

"Yes," she said. "And that's a darn shame. You know, Keith, you have that fire burning in you, too. And someday you'll find someone who brings it out in you. I'm sorry it wasn't me, and I'm sorry I led you to believe it could be by accepting your proposal. I'm sorry if the wedding being cancelled has caused you any embarrassment."

"Sanderson said you gave him notice," he said, awkward with this discussion of passion, awkward with her apology. "What are you going to do?"

"I'm going to see what I need to do to get accredited as a teacher."

She braced herself for the blast of his scorn, but instead he regarded her thoughtfully. "I think you'd make a great teacher, Lacey. What made you cut your hair? It makes you look different. Like a whole different person. Like a little tomboy looking for a fight. Reckless."

"I cut my hair because I need my life to be about what I want instead of about what other people want from me."

"Lacey, I hope you find whatever you are looking for. And I mean that from the bottom of my heart."

"Thank you."

She watched him go, closing the door quietly behind him.

Ethan regarded his plate. It looked like heaven. A fluffy mountain of white, whipped potatoes, rivers of rich brown gravy running off them, two thick slices of cooked-to-perfection beef, peas in cream sauce.

He took a bite and refused to meet Gumpy's angry glare. Why did everything Mrs. Justin cooked look so good and taste so...bland?

Danny and Doreen were building volcanoes out of their

spuds. Mrs. Justin scolded them, but they ignored her. They had been pretending for the past few days that they did not understand English.

"Aggie," Gumpy said, "it's a good thing you can square dance, because you ain't much of a cook."

Mrs. Justin sniffed, but a little blush moved up her wrinkled neck.

Just what I need, Ethan thought, a geriatric romance under my roof.

"If I find you a recipe, will you at least try the chicken gumbo stuff?" Gumpy demanded.

"I could try, I guess."

Gumpy grinned toothlessly at her, but swallowed his grin as soon as he looked at Ethan. Ethan was on the receiving end of only black looks these days. As if it was his fault Lacey's father had had a heart attack.

The atmosphere at the table was so heavy he was glad when the phone rang.

He started to get up. Then wondered if it was her. She called every other night to talk to the twins. She hadn't asked to speak to him.

And he hadn't asked to speak to her.

A man had some pride.

Gumpy said the engagement was off and seemed to expect him to leap on the first plane after her, but he couldn't bring himself to do it.

He had asked for his sign from the heavens. He hadn't come first in the bull riding. He'd come second. He had to live with that. It wasn't meant to be.

Nobody else was getting up to answer the phone, either.

He finally gave in. It was his sister.

"Ethan, Danny and Doreen just sound despondent every time I talk to them lately." The line crackled, and her voice faded and then came back. "Andrew and I have agreed I should come back there. I'm going to fly in to Calgary on Tuesday. Things are under control here. In a month or so I should be able to bring Danny and Doreen home."

He felt the bottom fall out of his heart.

No Lacey.

No twins.

What was life going to be like? Quiet. Plain. Dull. Without laughter.

"You'll want to tell them the good news yourself," he said, and it didn't even sound as though he had a lump in his throat. "Hang on, and I'll get them."

He put the twins on the phone, went to the back porch and got his jacket. It was bitterly cold out. It was probably gorgeous in California.

He walked down to the barn and checked the cattle and his horses. Stars spangled the inky blackness of the sky. His breath formed icy clouds when he exhaled.

After a while he sensed he was no longer alone. "Hi, Gumpy."

Gumpy emerged from the darkness. "The phone rang as soon as the twins hung up with their mom."

It was Lacey, and she had wanted to talk to him.

"I'm going to start my tour of the high schools next month." Gumpy said.

Great. No Lacey. No twins. No Gumpy. Ethan couldn't even trust himself to speak. He looked desperately for a bright spot in the suddenly bleak landscape of his life.

No more Mrs. Justin's cooking.

"I guess you'll want me to move my stuff." Gumpy came up beside him and hooked his boot on the fence. "I won't be working here no more."

"Gumpy, you don't just work here. You know that.

Your ancestors owned this land, just like mine. It belongs to you as much as to me. Besides, I'm kind of attached to you, God knows why." His voice low, he added, "I hope you'll always consider this home."

Gumpy nodded, clearly satisfied. "When I first came here, you could not have said these things."

"You're a good teacher, Grandfather."

"I know it."

The silence stretched between them, the stars winked above them.

Finally, Gumpy spoke again. "If there's going to be a wedding, you should do it while your sister's home. It costs a lot of money to fly back and forth from Rotanbonga."

"A wedding? Between who? You and *Aggie?*"

"Is your heart telling you the wedding is going to be between me and Aggie?" Gumpy asked quietly.

"My heart isn't telling me nothing."

"Then you aren't listening to it."

"I asked for a sign," he blurted out. "If I won first place in the bull-riding event, I was going to ask her if she might think of staying. Maybe, someday, you know—"

Gumpy stared at him, aghast. "A sign?"

"Somehow, I thought you'd approve."

"You foolish young pup."

Ethan glared at him, but after a moment started to laugh softly. "Gumpy, that woman made me feel like I didn't know whether I was coming or going. Imagine a grown man letting the outcome of a rodeo event determine what he's going to do with his life."

Gumpy reached into his pocket and pulled out a crumpled piece of paper. "Aggie found this under her bed."

He handed it to Ethan.

Ethan looked at it. He read:

ride horses
be a teacher
have babies
go to a rodeo
swim naked
dance
laugh more
make mistakes
take chances

Something had been crossed out. Furiously. He squinted and read through the pen marks.

kiss Ethan

His heart was beating furiously in his chest. She wanted to have babies. The thought of her and him having babies together made him weak with wanting.

And bonus, they had to make the babies first.

Maybe he shouldn't be jumping to conclusions. Wanting to kiss him was different from wanting him to be a part of this list with her, sharing her whole life with him.

But then he thought of that night, which seemed like such an unbearably long time ago, when they had danced.

And she had offered.

Not her body. How could he have been so stupid?

Her soul. Her life. She had offered him everything she was.

And he had walked away. No wonder she had hopped a plane back to California. It probably didn't have a bloody thing to do with her dad's heart.

"What are you going to do about it?" Gumpy asked softly.

And suddenly he knew. He felt as though he'd been sitting in the doldrums, and a flicker of a breeze touched the sails within him. Began to fill his heart.

"I'm going to go see her," he said. He folded her list carefully. "I think I need to return this to her."

Gumpy nodded. "If you go quick, I can come, too."

"What for?" Ethan asked suspiciously.

"I ain't never been to California. I want to see Mystery Lodge at Knott's Berry Farm."

"Lacey."

Lacey looked up. Her secretary, Kelly, had a huge flat box in her arms.

"This just came for you." Kelly sat the bulky parcel on a chair. "How's your arm?"

Lacey had tried out a horse yesterday afternoon and fallen off. She didn't care. She was trying another one tonight.

Once, she had thought she had been given ten days to live life to the fullest. Now she realized that all of life was meant to be lived to the fullest. Not just ten days.

And it didn't matter if it did feel as though your heart was breaking. No excuses. You hit the dirt, you brushed it off, and you went on. Living. Really living. Feeling things intensely. Sadness, but joy, too. Life had to be about more than going through the motions.

"My arm's fine."

"You should have seen the guy who delivered this package," Kelly said.

Lacey glanced up at Kelly. Her plump face was flushed prettily. "Two ax handles wide?" she guessed.

Kelly nodded, giggled and left, pulling the door shut behind her.

Lacey tried to go back to work, but work was so difficult right now. Sometimes she wondered how she had ever managed to do it. It was depressing sorting through the debris of people's lives.

She closed her eyes and rubbed the bridge of her nose. Was the worry furrow smaller? It seemed to be. Strangely, she could smell the inside of Gumpy's tepee. That wonderful smell of smoke and leather.

She imagined herself sitting there, and remembered the lesson she had learned that night. That her heart, her desire, would lead her to her true self. She breathed deeply, astounded that the aroma was all around her, astounded by how peaceful she felt. In her imagination, she was wearing that magnificent buckskin dress, and Ethan was sitting across the fire from her, in a simple, fringed buckskin shirt.

Her eyes clicked open. The smell was real. Leather and smoke.

She got up from her desk so fast, she knocked over her chair. Her heart began to pound as she approached the package. She bent and inhaled.

The beautiful smell of wood smoke and cured leather filled her nostrils.

With trembling hands she undid the package strings and took off the lid.

Her heart stopped beating, and her eyes filled with tears.

Her hands shaking uncontrollably, she reached out and reverently touched the soft leather of the dress. Ethan's mother's dress.

No. That wasn't quite right.

Ethan's bride's dress. She gathered it up and pressed

it against herself. Then she raced for the door of her office. "Kelly! Where—"

She stopped.

He was there.

Two ax handles wide. Sitting on the corner of her secretary's desk, one long leg anchoring him to the ground, the other swinging carelessly.

"Oh," she said. "Hi."

He got up. His eyes, beautiful and gray and still, locked on hers. Kelly was watching breathlessly.

"What are you doing here?" she said, clutching the dress.

"I was in the neighborhood."

"You were not. This is not a neighborhood you would ever be in."

"Gumpy had a sudden hankering to see Mystery Lodge."

"Why did you give me the dress?"

"Oh. That."

Kelly was nearly falling off her chair.

"Get in here," she said, opening her door wider.

He passed by her, and she shut the door. Almost before it shut, he had her in his arms and was kissing her all over. With passion. And wanting. And tenderness. And welcome.

And homecoming.

He kissed her as if he were a soldier who had been away too long. A sailor. A frontiersman. An explorer.

She kissed him back as if she were the woman who had waited. Scanning the hills and the horizon. Praying and hoping.

"Ethan," she breathed. "Oh, God, Ethan, kiss me."

He complied and then whispered something in her ear about swimming that made her turn crimson.

"You found my list!" she said accusingly.

"Yes, ma'am."

"Is that why you came?"

"I told you. Gumpy had to see Mystery Lodge."

"Is that where he is now?"

"Actually, he's at the hospital."

"The hospital? Nothing's wrong with him, is there?"

"Nah. He was getting to know your dad."

"My dad?" she whispered.

"He insisted I get your dad's blessing before I came here. You know Gumpy. Old-fashioned and newfangled all at the same time."

"My dad's blessing for what?"

Ethan ignored the question. "Looked like he was planning on staying for a while. Your dad was kind of a captive audience. When I left Gumpy was explaining to him how there are too many chemicals in today's food, too much processing."

He kissed her on the end of her nose, which made it hard for her to focus on the conversation. Were they talking about her dad's blessing?

"And he was telling him Mother Earth's soil had been depleted of essential elements."

"Is that a Native belief?"

"I think it was pretty much pure Gumpy. He was telling him he'd have him fixed up in no time, though."

"How? Is he going to do some ancient Native healing?"

Ethan shook his head. "Nutritional supplements."

She laughed. "Okay. Let's get to the part about my dad's blessing and this dress."

He kissed her on the nose again. She wished he'd stop. It was very distracting. Or at least he should move to her lips.

"Did you know your dad has always wanted to fly fish?"

"My dad?"

Ethan nodded. "Gumpy promised to take him. When he comes to visit us."

"Us?"

"You and me."

"You and me?"

"What did you think I asked your dad's blessing for? For Gumpy to see Knott's Berry Farm?"

She was holding the dress so tight her knuckles turned white. "You and me what, Ethan?"

He looked at her solemnly and then said softly, "You and me. Riding horses together, teaching each other, having babies, going to rodeos, swimming naked, dancing, laughing, making mistakes. Taking chances. Together. Forever."

"Oh, Ethan."

"If you say yes, that is."

"Ethan, yes."

"I haven't even asked the question yet."

"Yes." She kissed him. On the throat.

"Lacey—"

"Yes!" She nibbled his ears.

"Will you—"

"Yes!" She kissed his cheeks and touched his eyelids with her fingertips.

"Marry me?"

"A thousand times, yes." She took his lips with hers. She tasted him and knew what forever tasted like. She gazed up into his eyes and saw the love and tenderness in them and knew what forever looked like.

"Do you think, uh, you want to take my name? When we get married?"

"Of course."

"Oh, God."

"What?"

"I'm afraid I can picture you in lacy black. All too well."

She laughed and blushed and laughed again.

The smell of smoke and leather danced in the air between them.

She looked again into his eyes and saw, in the way she was reflected, her true self. And his.

She smiled with soft delight, and Ethan touched her cheek, leaned close to her, groaned, and gathered her tightly in his arms. He whispered against her hair something about having all he ever needed for joy.

She closed her eyes and let herself melt into him. And again, in her imagination, she wore the dress and he wore a buckskin shirt.

They were in the yard in front of the ranch house, the snow sparkling with a million diamonds as the sun hit it.

Gumpy stood beside him, and the twins stood beside her. There was his sister and his mother and his father. She recognized them from pictures. There was her father and mother, too. The space was crowded with ranchers and Native people and even lawyers from her firm.

They were gathered to celebrate the power of love. Joy seemed to shimmer in the very air. Lacey felt such an incredible sense of connection, a lack of barriers, a sense of community. A sense of continuity. Of love passing from one generation to the next, of love going on forever.

Of love healing everything if it were only given the chance.

And her eyes moved to the ridge, where she and Ethan had ridden that day a long time ago. And even in her imagination she gasped softly.

For he was there. Ethan's ancestor. And his woman.

They were absolutely magnificent. Free. Black piercing eyes, black hair long and untamed.

And his ancestor raised his lance to them, in benediction, in blessing, and then warrior and bride turned and rode away.

*   *   *   *   *

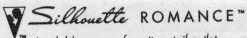

If you enjoyed what you just read,
then we've got an offer you can't resist!

Take 2 bestselling
love stories FREE!
Plus get a FREE surprise gift!

Of all the unforgettable families created by
#1 *New York Times* bestselling author

NORA ROBERTS

the Donovans are the most extraordinary. For, along with
their irresistible appeal, they've inherited some rather
remarkable gifts from their Celtic ancestors.

Coming in November 1999

THE DONOVAN LEGACY

3 full-length novels in one special volume:

CAPTIVATED: Hardheaded skeptic Nash Kirkland has *always*
kept his feelings in check, until he falls under the bewitching
spell of mysterious Morgana Donovan.

ENTRANCED: Desperate to find a missing child, detective
Mary Ellen Sutherland dubiously enlists beguiling
Sebastian Donovan's aid and discovers his uncommon abilities
include a talent for seduction.

CHARMED: Enigmatic healer Anastasia Donovan would do
anything to save the life of handsome Boone Sawyer's
daughter, even if it means revealing her secret to the man
who'd stolen her heart.

Also in November 1999 from Silhouette Intimate Moments

ENCHANTED

Lovely, guileless Rowan Murray is drawn to darkly enigmatic
Liam Donovan with a power she's never imagined possible. But
before Liam can give Rowan his love, he must first reveal to
her his incredible secret.

▼ *Silhouette* ®
™

Available at your favorite retail outlet.

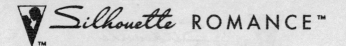

Silhouette ROMANCE™

Join *Silhouette Romance*
as more couples experience
the joy only babies
can bring!

Bundles of Joy

September 1999
THE BABY BOND
by Lilian Darcy (SR #1390)

Tom Callahan a daddy? Impossible! Yet that was before Julie Gregory showed up
with the shocking news that she carried his child. Now the father-to-be knew
marriage was the answer!

October 1999
BABY, YOU'RE MINE
by Lindsay Longford (SR #1396)

Marriage was the *last* thing on Murphy Jones's mind when he invited
beautiful—and pregnant—Phoebe McAllister to stay with him. But then
she and her newborn bundle filled his house with laughter...and had bachelor
Murphy rethinking his no-strings lifestyle....

And in December 1999, popular author

MARIE FERRARELLA

brings you

THE BABY BENEATH THE MISTLETOE (SR #1408)

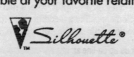

Available at your favorite retail outlet.

Silhouette®

COMING NEXT MONTH

#1408 THE BABY BENEATH THE MISTLETOE—Marie Ferrarella
Bundles of Joy

Natural-born nurturer Michelle Rozanski wasn't about to let Tony Marino face instant fatherhood alone. Even if Tony could be gruffer than a hibernating bear, he'd made a place in his home—and heart—for an abandoned child. And now if Michelle had her way, they'd *never* face parenthood alone!

#1409 EXPECTING AT CHRISTMAS—Charlotte Maclay

When his butler was away, the *last* replacement millionaire Griffin Jones expected was eight-months-pregnant Loretta Santana. Yet somehow she'd charmed him into hiring her. And now this confirmed bachelor found himself falling for Loretta...and her Christmas-baby-on-the-way....

#1410 EMMA AND THE EARL—Elizabeth Harbison
Cinderella Brides

She thought she'd outgrown dreams of happily-ever-after, yet when American Emma Lawrence found herself a guest of Earl Brice Palliser's lavish estate, he seemed her very own Prince Charming come to life. But was there a place in Brice's noble heart for plain Emma?

#1411 A DIAMOND FOR KATE—Moyra Tarling

The moment devastatingly handsome Dr. Marshall Diamond entered the hospital, nurse Kate Turner recognized him as the man she'd secretly loved as a child. But could Kate convince him that the girl from his past was now a woman he could trust...forever?

#1412 THE MAN, THE RING, THE WEDDING—Patricia Thayer
With These Rings

Tall, dark and *rich* John Rossi was cozying up to innocent Angelina Covelli for one reason—revenge. But old family feuds weren't sweet enough to keep the sexy CEO fixed on his goal. His mind—and heart—kept steering him to Angelina...and rings...and weddings!

#1413 THE MILLIONAIRE'S PROPOSITION—Natalie Patrick

Waitress Becky Taylor was tempted to accept Clark Winstead's proposal. It was an enticing offer—a handsome millionaire, a rich life, family. If only it wasn't lacking a few elements...like a wedding...and love. Good thing Becky was planning to do a little enticing of her own....

CMN1199